The Adve ̄ ̄ ̄ ̄₁

WHITEBEARD

Enjoy the adventure!

M.C.P. Seniel

The Adventures of
WHITEBEARD

Book One

M.C.D. Etheridge

Illustrated by Olivia Ong

FLASH KNIGHT

INTRODUCING ...

Dasher

Dancer

Prancer

Vixen

FLASH KNIGHT

Published by Flash Knight Productions.
First published 2018
Text copyright © M.C.D. Etheridge, 2018

Illustrations copyright © Olivia Ong, 2018

ISBN: 978-0-6483590-0-5

Book cover designed by Megan Sheer featuring illustrations
by Olivia Ong.

Edited by Tegan Morrison.

Printed and bound by IngramSpark.

www.flashknight.com

To those who give

Prologue

Close your eyes, open your ears
And imagine a Christmas Eve.
This festive tale begins at sea,
Where it ends, you won't believe.

It's the story of the man we know
As the loving Santa Claus.
How long ago, a saltwater thief,
He pirated these shores.

For once upon a time, my friends,
He was a man children feared.
Back then, all knew this ocean rogue
As pirate Captain Whitebeard.

Upon his ship, the *Rudolph's Revenge*,
He prowled the ocean deep.
Back then, as now, awaiting him
Would keep you from your sleep.

No gifts had he to offer
As his ship sailed in on yours.
He'd steal aboard and help himself
To all your booty, loot and stores.

His faithful gang of pirates
Were always by his side.
Guns, pistols and cutlasses drawn,
They sailed upon every tide.

Now half you know already:
Dasher, Dancer, Prancer and Vixen.
The crew completing this piece of eight:
Comet, Cupid, Donner and Blitzen.

So there you have Whitebeard's clan
Aboard the *Rudolph's Revenge*.
Out in search of prey each night,
Meet them, meet unfortunate end!

More ruthless than Captain Morgan,
More rake than Francis Drake.
It was all take, no give in those days,
Of that make no mistake.

Can this really be Father Christmas?
Can this really be our Saint?
'It's not Santa Claus!' I hear you cry.
'It's not, can't be, it ain't!'

Well it is, my little dearios.
Nicholas wasn't always good.
Long before he was canonised,
Cannons sounded where he stood.

For of children he's a patron saint,
But of thieves and sailors too.
And by the time this story's done,
You'll know it to be true.

Chapter 1

Packed full of gunpowder, the giant Christmas pudding was about to explode.

This part of the plan had gone perfectly for the pirates. It was a triumph.

There was just one small problem. A tiny detail really, but one they couldn't escape …

The pirates were still inside!

'Why on earth did we agree to this?' asked a teenage pirate dressed in black. 'This was never going to work.'

'We're not done for yet, Dasher,' replied the cabin boy. His cherub-like face lit up. 'The captain will save us!'

'Don't be stupid, Cupid,' said Dasher. 'We're doomed. Honestly, you're such an optometrist!'

'I think you mean optimist,' corrected a dusky girl pirate. 'Optimists are hopeful people who look on the bright side of life. Optometrists are doctors who look at people's eyes. Maybe you should see one, to save us all from your unbearable hindsight.'

'Very funny, Vixen. You know what's not funny? How you got us into this horrible mess in the first place. I don't know why we ever let a girl on the *Rudolph's Revenge* anyway.'

'Cool it, Dasher,' said Dancer, who appeared to be wearing a patchwork of colourful flags. 'How were we supposed to know they'd set fire to the pudding? Ain't no use in blaming anyone now.'

'I blame the mermaids,' said Comet, screwing up his nose.

'I blame the trolls,' blurted the bulky Blitzen, taking up most of the room inside the pudding.

'I blame the witch,' said Prancer, smoothing his immaculate hair.

'No, Dasher's right,' said Vixen, frowning. 'This *is* my fault. Now let me think. There's a way out of this yet.'

But time was not on the pirates' side. Trapped in the belly of the giant Christmas pudding, with its deadly use-by-date almost up, their hearts hammered away to the beat of a ticking clock …

Given the nightmare the pirates now found themselves in, it was hard to believe that just 24 hours earlier they were happily celebrating Christmas Eve the best way pirates know how … with a daring raid on another ship.

From his favourite spot on the *Rudolph's Revenge*, high up in the crow's nest, Cupid was first to see it sailing across the turquoise waters of the Caribbean.

The joy of finally spotting a ship to attack raced through every inch of his scrawny frame.

'Sails ahoy!' he shouted.

Cupid's shipmates looked up as he leapt down, the wind rushing through his mop of blonde curls as he swung like a monkey to land on deck.

In his excitement he sprinted past Prancer and Vixen at the sails, jumped over one of Blitzen's cannon and bumped Comet at the ship's wheel, almost knocking off Comet's spectacles.

'I say, old chap, do be careful,' said Comet, peering over the rim of his half-moon glasses.

'Sorry, Mister Comet, but there are sails!'

The door to the captain's cabin burst open and out stepped an ancient mariner with a magnificent white beard.

'Sails you say, me lad?' he boomed.

The jolly-looking fellow smiled more with his eyes than his mouth, which was hidden by white whiskers. The old man had done so much sailing in his time that his sunburnt skin was covered in wrinkles, each line mapping another adventure. Upon his wavy white hair sat a tricorn hat, which matched his brown buccaneer boots. A splendid red jacket buttoned up over his well-fed belly, but only just. Tucked into his belt he carried two shining flintlock pistols and at his side hung a large cutlass.

'Well, my boy,' said Captain Whitebeard, taking out his spyglass. 'What d'ya see now?'

Cupid pointed and there, as the sun began to sink in the late afternoon sky, was a tall ship.

The captain lifted his spyglass to his eye, grinned and snapped it shut.

'Two shares to our young Cupid here for spotting her,' he said, ruffling the boy's hair. 'It appears we've a Spanish ship in our sights, and don't she look like pretty prey? Aye, it's Christmas Eve and with the sailors swimming in grog, she'll be easy enough to take. They'll be feasting on all kinds of delicious Spanish food. Tasty tapas. Roast turkey. Smoked pork. They really lay it on, you know. I think nutty nougat is their speciality at Christmas, but we may even get a mince pie too if we're lucky. No more sprouts for us!'

The pirates cheered as their tummies rumbled. They hadn't spotted a ship to attack for weeks and all they had left to eat was a barrel of smelly old Brussels sprouts. Even worse, the diet meant the crew's bottoms were tooting out some of the nastiest smells known to man. It was so gassy below deck, they couldn't even light candles for fear of blowing a hole in the side of the ship.

'Ho, ho, ho,' laughed Whitebeard, licking his lips. 'Oh yes, our Christmas will be merry indeed!'

Little did the captain know, the attack that night would spark a chain of events to change Christmas as we know it, forever.

Chapter 2

'Dancer, quickly if you please,' said Whitebeard. 'The Spanish colours!'

'Aye, aye, Captain!' replied Dancer, springing forward with a jig.

Dancer was the ship's Master of Disguise. This was a handy skill to have when your job involved tricking and robbing people. His other responsibility was to look after all the flags. When they spotted a British ship, they'd fly the Union Jack to get nice and close. If it was French, up went the French colours. Often Dancer had to produce a flag so quickly he'd started wearing them as his own clothes. A patchwork of colour, Dancer looked rather like a pantomime character. He was currently

wearing the Spanish flag as his underpants and whipped them off as quickly as he could to run up the mast.

'Excellent work, Dancer, that should fool them,' said Whitebeard happily. 'Here's the plan. We're going to pretend to be Spanish sailors and sail right alongside them. Now, who knows how to say "Merry Christmas" in Spanish?'

The crew looked at each other blankly.

'*Feliz Navidad!*' said Vixen.

'Very good, Vixen. Smart as gunpowder, you are.'

'Teacher's pet,' said Prancer.

'Shut up,' said Vixen, blushing.

It was unusual for girls to sail on pirate ships in those days as most crews thought that having a girl on board was bad luck. But the clever Vixen was a great sailor and had brought nothing but good fortune to the crew.

'We'll sail as fast as we can to catch her,' continued Whitebeard. 'Then once we're within earshot, we'll all shout out "Fleas Nanny-Dad".'

'*Feliz Navidad,*' corrected Vixen.

'Exactly. They'll think that we too are Spanish sailors coming to celebrate this fine Christmas Eve. Then, when we're safely aboard, we'll show our true colours and shout and pull our most horrible faces to scare them half to death. They won't know what to do but hand over all the loot they have. What say you to that, me hearties?'

This fired up the crew no end and they all began practising their horrible faces. The award for Most Horrible Face easily went to the ship's hairy cook, Donner. His bushy black beard looked like the business end of a broomstick and he had enough scars on his olive cheeks to play a game of noughts and crosses. Even his mouth was so full of gold teeth it was like staring into Aladdin's cave. It's fair to say, Donner had a face only a mother could love.

'Dasher, Dancer, prepare to board her,' commanded Whitebeard. 'Prancer, Vixen, prepare the sails, we must catch her before night falls. Donner, Blitzen, ready the guns. Steady as she goes, Comet and Cupid, don't let her out of your sight.'

'Aye aye, Captain,' sang out the crew, and if you think your home looks busy on Christmas Eve, that's nothing compared to the hive of activity on board the *Rudolph's Revenge*.

Cupid ran up front and perched himself between the antlers on the figurehead at the ship's bow, keeping a lookout.

Mastering the helm was Comet, Whitebeard's trusted navigator. Even though he'd been booted out of the Royal Navy, he was an excellent sailor and had an ocean of sea smarts. Steering the vessel towards the Spanish ship, he called for his shipmates to release more sail.

'You'll never catch me, Vixen,' teased Prancer, winking in her direction.

'The only rope you'll ever beat me to is the one they put around your neck,' replied Vixen, springing to another set of ropes and leaving him for dust.

Vixen's tongue was as quick as her sea craft and no one was the target of her cutting jibes more than her rival, Prancer. In his expensive red waistcoat, Prancer fancied himself rotten and, to be honest, he loved the attention. Vixen and Prancer smiled with satisfaction as the sails billowed with a fresh gust of wind and propelled them towards their prey.

An ocean-going Bermuda sloop, the *Rudolph's Revenge* was fast; few ships could match her for speed. As she closed in on the Spanish vessel, her triangular mainsail cut across the water like the fin of a shark moving in for the kill.

Blitzen was on deck and prepared the firepower. Twice the size of most men and with hands as big as wheelbarrows, he could easily juggle up to ten cannonballs at once. But alas, Blitzen was thicker than two short planks and relied on his best mate Donner to steer him in the right direction.

'Release the powder monkeys, Blitzen,' said Donner, in his thick Turkish accent.

With only a bag of peanuts, Donner had trained a troop of Madagascan monkeys to help Blitzen fire the eight cannon on deck. Donner had once been a master gunner himself, until his left leg was smashed to pieces by a cannonball. Now Donner spent most of his time hobbling around in the galley kitchen, but when it came to action he always assisted Blitzen with the guns. Both his crutch and peg made excellent ramrods. Together, Donner and Blitzen were almost as impressive with the guns as Prancer and Vixen were at the sails.

Dasher 'The Blade' (a nickname he'd given himself) was a swordsman of the sea. The very devil with a rapier, the boy in black was Whitebeard's finest fighting man and could best more than a dozen foes at once. For that alone, the rest of the crew put up with both the amount of time he spent in the bathroom and his personality, which was pricklier than a hedgehog's sideburns.

'You could have helped me, Dasher,' puffed Dancer, returning with the large sea chest.

Dasher scowled as Dancer emptied the contents of the chest onto the deck. Rummaging through the pile of red soldiers' coats, blue ballgowns and fancy French wigs, he eventually found what he was looking for.

'Here we are, Captain,' said Dancer. 'The finest collection of Spanish mustachios this side of Madrid.'

'Ho ho ho,' laughed Whitebeard. 'Bravo, Dancer! They'll do the trick, to be sure!'

Chapter 3

Now you may think Whitebeard a wretched wrong'un, and, well, you may be right. But upon the seas there sailed a man to really give you a fright. If Whitebeard kept you awake at night and stole you from your dreams, Jack Frost appeared in your worst nightmares. For where Whitebeard tricked his victims to get what he wanted, Captain Frost delivered on his terrible threats.

If you dared to look at old Frosty – and you'd be braver than most if you did – the first thing you'd notice was the black eye-patch covering his left eye. In a duel with Whitebeard, the villain had lost half his sight. From that day on, Jack Frost swore to find his arch-enemy.

'An eye for an eye ain't enough for me,' he'd vowed. 'Whitebeard's death will be painfully slow.'

Just to look at Captain Frost would send a shiver down your spine. Dressed in his white coat, hat and breeches, the man looked like a living ghost. Even his face was ghoulishly thin and pale; his cruel features jutting out like icicles. Aye, he was the most heartless pirate that ever lived, you can count on that.

Jack Frost's ship, the *Frostbite*, was a huge galleon and easily the largest ship to pirate the seas back in the Golden Age of Piracy. Armed with 40 fearsome guns, to hear his cannon sounding was to hear the ocean roar. The enormous size of Frosty's ship meant he needed hundreds of men to handle her, and he had them in droves.

From his position on the top deck, Jack Frost looked down on his cutthroat crew. The decks were crawling with swarthy sea rovers, tattooed tars and marauding mercenaries.

Big, burly, British buccaneers battened down the hatches.

Drunk Dutchmen diced.

Sangria-soaked Spanish swordsmen swayed and sang sea shanties.

Freebooting French filibusters flogged galley slaves.

Prussian pikemen poked at pickled pork roasting away in the fiery flames of a giant spit.

Angry Amazon tribesmen, with clubs the size of tree trunks, traded insults with Incas who used poison darts, coated in the venom of the deadliest frogs on earth, to settle their scores.

And not one of them ever wrote to their mothers.

Rascals rotten to the core this lot and every last one of them was hell-bent on rampaging the Spanish colonies and seeking out Whitebeard so their captain might have his revenge.

Back up on the top deck, two men, a small weasel of a man and a lanky youth with greasy hair, approached Jack Frost with news.

''Scuse us, Captain,' said the small man with a cockney accent.

'Yes, Oggin, what is it? Can't you see I'm busy looting the Christmas cards we stole last week. Oh look, a fiver.'

'Yes, sir, 'pologies, sir, but there's news on the *Rudolph's Revenge*.'

'Well, out with it.'

Oggin nudged the greasy youth standing beside him. 'Go on, Finch,' he prompted.

'Beggin' your pardon, sir, but a few minutes ago I spotted the *Revenge* sailing windward towards another ship.'

'Are you quite sure?' demanded Frost, giving the youth his full attention.

'Aye, Captain, it was the *Revenge* all right,' said Finch.

Oggin winced at the youth's choice of words. It was well known that Jack Frost was a bit sensitive about the eye he'd lost and insisted his crew *never* utter the words 'Aye, Captain'.

'WHAT did you say?'

A terrified Finch shook his head. 'Nothing, Captain,' he mumbled.

'Spanker, come here,' bellowed Frost. A muscular man with a paddle stepped forward.

'Nooooo,' pleaded Finch. 'Not another spanking. It's been weeks since the last one and I've only just managed to sit down without bursting a blister. Please, sir, I'll never say that word again.'

'Very well, young man. You won't have to worry about sitting down ...'

'Thank you, sir.'

'But I hope you can swim!'

With a nod to his henchmen, two brutes stepped forward, picked up the terrified young pirate and cast him headfirst over the side of the ship. There was a scream followed by a loud splash.

'Set a course, Oggin, and be off with you,' said Frost, tearing open another envelope with his dagger.

'Yes, sir, fank you, sir.'

Oh yes, Frosty by name, frosty by nature,

and with his mean collection of cutthroats armed to their icy teeth, the villains aboard the *Frostbite* sailed on, ready to sink their fangs into fresh victims.

Chapter 4

As the sun set with a crimson glow, a friendly chorus of 'Feliz Navidad' greeted the *Rudolph's Revenge* as it sailed alongside the Spanish ship. Whitebeard's pirates smiled behind their big black moustaches. The plan was working perfectly. They broke into a few chuckles as Vixen babbled away to one of the Spanish officers in her best attempt at a deep, male voice. No one quite knew what she was saying, but it was very entertaining.

'Right, Captain, there's good news and bad news,' began Vixen, turning to her shipmates.

'What's the good news?' asked Whitebeard, waving merrily at the Spanish crew.

'The good news is they believe our story; that we're taking a stash of silver back to Spain.

Captain Caganer of the *Ave Maria* warmly welcomes you and me aboard his ship, to share in a festive toast. Also, the good captain will gladly accept our offer of a gift.'

'Wonderful work, Vixen,' said Whitebeard. 'Now, what's the bad news?'

'The bad news is we must go aboard unarmed.'

'Ah, well, we half expected as much. Right, Prancer, Blitzen, be ready to help us with the treasure chest we're taking aboard as a Christmas present. The rest of you, you know what to do. Mister Comet, await my signal. You're in charge of the *Rudolph's Revenge* until I return. Be ready, friends. This is the tricky part.'

With Dancer's marvellous moustaches firmly attached to their lips, Whitebeard and Vixen made their way on to the *Ave Maria*. Aboard the Spanish ship, it was all cheer and merriment. The Spanish sailors swilled their goblets and danced jovial jigs to fast fiddles and clacking castanets. None were the wiser to our pirates' plan.

Whitebeard and Vixen were led to the top deck where Captain Caganer nodded his greeting. A proud man, the captain did little to welcome his guests and stood with an entitled sneer as he awaited the arrival of his Christmas present. After exchanging the briefest of courtesies, Vixen called for Prancer and Blitzen to bring up the gift.

Leading the way with the heavy treasure chest, Blitzen's enormous size caught the attention of the Spanish sailors mid jig. Even the fiddlers stopped playing to gape at the giant. In the silence, two Spaniards approached Blitzen, taking in his striped t-shirt, gold earrings and anchor tattoo. They knew there was something not quite right about this man, but for the life of them, they couldn't put their finger on it.

One of the sailors began talking to Blitzen, but he spoke with such alarming speed the big man couldn't make out a single word said. As the other sailor prodded the treasure chest, nerves got to Blitzen and he let out an outrageous blast from his bottom. The sprouty smell was enough to send the Spaniards reeling and for a second Prancer thought the game was up. But the thundering noise had broken the silence and the drunken sailors laughed hysterically and slapped Blitzen on the back to cries of '*Feliz Navidad!*'

The fiddlers started up again and the celebration continued.

'Feels-Nappy-Bad!' shouted Blitzen happily.

'For crying out loud,' whispered Prancer, 'stop blowing our cover!'

With great care, Blitzen and Prancer placed the treasure chest under Caganer's long nose and the captain nodded approvingly for drinks to be served. Whitebeard was so pleased to receive a refreshing Christmas punch, he almost tore it from the steward's hand.

'*Salud,*' he said, smashing it against Caganer's glass.

Whitebeard gulped down his drink in seconds. Then, forgetting all about his enormous fake moustache, he wiped his mouth and pulled half of the black tash from his lip. It drooped from his face like a stray sock hanging from a laundry basket. Aghast, Vixen saw it immediately and coughed a loud hint to her captain.

It was too late. Caganer had seen it too, but before he could raise the alarm, Whitebeard kicked the chest at his feet. The lid sprang open to reveal Cupid training a crossbow squarely between the Spanish captain's eyes. The cabin boy lifted a finger to his lips to insist on silence.

'Do not move or make a sound, Captain,' said Whitebeard, adjusting his tash. 'Just smile as if the contents of this chest are as dear to you as life itself. For, funnily enough, that's precisely its value.'

The words Captain Caganer said at that moment are quite unrepeatable, but let's just say the Spaniard had nothing nice to say about Whitebeard or his dear old mum.

'Neptune's noggin!' said Whitebeard. 'I never knew my mother, but if she were here today I'm sure she would compliment you on your English, sir.'

'I do not speak good English, you dog,' replied Caganer. 'Everyone knows you learn the rude words first in any language.'

Whitebeard leaned in. 'Keep smiling, Captain,' he whispered. 'Now, perhaps you can teach me how to say "I surrender my ship". For if you do, I swear I will not harm a man aboard.'

'Here, let me make this decision easier for you,' said Prancer, pulling a pistol from the Spanish captain's belt and prodding it into his back.

'Now!' roared Whitebeard to his crew. 'Now, Dasher! Now, Dancer! Now, Prancer and Vixen! On, Comet! On, Cupid! On, Donner and Blitzen!'

From the *Rudolph's Revenge*, Comet signalled for Donner and the Madagascan powder monkeys to fire their cannon into the *Ave Maria*. Amid the smoke and soot, Dancer cast his grappling hook to catch a barb high above the Spanish mainsail. He swung in above the Spanish sailors and cut loose the sails which fell on top of the bumbling crew. Trapped beneath, there was little they could do but groan and moan and try to wrestle out from under the canvas. But whenever one emerged, Dancer swung down to knock him over the head with a belaying pin.

'Ho ho ho,' boomed Whitebeard. 'I am the feared pirate Captain Whitebeard. We have your ship. Do not resist us, or else!'

Stunned by the pirate raid, the Spanish sailors were little match for Blitzen who had a knockout left fist. The giant hit them so hard, the Spaniards flew backwards. Those who avoided getting hit desperately tried to find the stash of pistols they'd left on deck for this very reason.

But it was no use, Dasher was right beside them, swirling rapier in hand. He cut the air with such a satisfying swish the sailors dared not make another move. The only one who did was quickly dealt with by Donner, who used his crutch to demonstrate an impressive golf swing and knocked the sailor clean off his feet.

Celebrating their victory, Whitebeard's pirates jeered and cheered and pulled their most horrible faces. A sailor standing next to Donner fainted instantly.

The Spanish captain looked defeated. 'She was right,' he snivelled.

'What?' asked Whitebeard. 'Who was right?'

'The witch!'

Chapter 5

Back onboard the *Frostbite*, Frosty's pirates caught sight of the action.

'Look, sir!' Oggin called to his master. 'Cannon ablaze to the starboard bow.'

'Excellent, Oggin, excellent,' said Jack Frost. 'How far off?'

'Not four leagues, sir. But the light is fadin'.'

'Very good, Oggin. You know what to do.'

'Fank you, sir.'

'Oggin?'

'Yes sir?'

'Why are you still here?'

'Well, sir, you know, it's Christmas. And, well, the lads and I have chipped in and we've got you a present.'

'Oggin!' said Frosty with a smile. 'You most certainly *should* have. But now is not the time, is it, you horrible little hedgepig?'

'Well, sir, if you don't mind me saying, sir. Now could be exactly the right time.'

'Very well, you foot-licking toad, but it better be good.'

'Yes, sir. This way, sir.' Oggin led his captain down the steps to the main deck where the men had gathered around a large present, the size of a caravan, wrapped in brown paper.

'Oooh, what could it be? Wait, don't tell me.'

Frosty rustled the giant box and heard a murmur from within. 'It's not more galley slaves, is it, Oggin?' asked Frosty with a sigh. 'Galley slaves were sooo last year.'

'No, sir, it's …'

'Wait!' said Frosty, giving the box another shake. He could have sworn he heard the sound of clashing blades. 'Oh, hang on a second! Oggin! No!? You really do know how to butter up your betters, don't you? It's that giant duelling octopus I've had my eye on these past months, isn't it? Oh, it'll be the perfect pet to put some holes into that white-bearded pumpkin.'

'No, sir, even better than that!'

Oggin gestured to his captain and Frosty tore away the paper, revealing the gift inside.

The captain stared.

'Well, sir,' said Oggin, looking down at his feet sheepishly. 'You see, what wiv so much sailin' this year, we really ain't had the chance to go out and buy you anyfin', so we've had to just f'row some'ing together wiv what we 'ad. Which in this case happens to be the Swiss Guards we defeated on that French warship a couple of months back.'

Frosty didn't move.

'But look, we've made some excellent modifications.'

'So you have, Oggin, so you have,' said Frosty. He was impressed. For there before him were a dozen zombified men dressed in the red, yellow and blue uniform of the Swiss Guard. But where

the fallen soldiers had lost a limb here and there, they'd been replaced with an array of viciously sharp blades.

'Allow me to introduce some of the men, sir,' said Oggin proudly. 'First we 'av Sawbones. This menace need only pull back this cord and his arm becomes a mechanised buzz saw. There'll be some sore bones when we let him loose on the enemy, sir.'

'Quite wonderful,' said Frosty.

'Next, we have Rabies. Now poor old Rabies' jaw was shot to pieces by our sharpshooters, so we've replaced it with these amazing gnashers. Now he can bite his way through just about anyfin'. Oh, and check out his claws. Ouch!'

'Ouch indeed, Oggin, ouch indeed.'

'Finally, meet Smith. As you can see, we've fitted his arm with a giant war hammer. Smith here will bash away at anyfin' like it's steel upon a blacksmith's anvil.'

'Smashing,' said Frosty with a cruel chuckle.

'Very good, sir,' said Oggin with a polite smile. 'Now, the rest of the troop are just kitted out wiv your standard blades. No hooks though. We thought that was a bit old school.'

'Oh, Oggin, I love them. Take an empty Christmas card from the pile over there.'

'Yes, sir, fank you, sir. Most kind.'

'I shall call them my "Swiss Army Knives",' said Frosty with a wicked grin.

'Very good, sir.'

'Now, my little pipsqueak, where's that mutton-chopped fool Whitebeard? I want to play with my new toys tonight!'

Chapter 6

Back aboard the *Ave Maria*, Christmas had come early for our pirates. The Spanish ship was a floating wooden palace, jam-packed with princely plunder. As Prancer and Vixen rounded up the last of the prisoners, the treasure hunt began. Dasher and Dancer headed to the cabins to look for loot, Donner and Blitzen checked the stores for food and Cupid made straight for the hold to discover the cargo.

Fastening the sorry sailors to the mast, Prancer winked at three Spanish beauties he'd found hidden in the captain's cabin.

'Leave the ladies alone, you rogue,' Whitebeard called to Prancer. 'I said tie them up, not chat them up!'

'Aye, Captain, yes, excuse me, sir,' said Prancer. 'I was just trying to find out where the señoritas keep their rubies and sapphires.'

'No you weren't,' said Vixen. 'It was "eyes like sapphires and lips like rubies". Honestly, your chat-up lines are enough to make me seasick.'

Although Vixen would never admit it, she'd sometimes get jealous when Prancer made eyes at other girls they met at sea. The ladies were always so finely dressed in their colourful gowns and petticoats. In her work slops and black buccaneer coat, Vixen just looked like one of the lads. She'd never worn a dress in her life and the only colour in her wardrobe was her purple headscarf. The trio of young ladies squealed as Vixen tightened the rope around their ankles an extra notch.

The first pirates to return on deck were Donner and Blitzen with news from the stores. 'Sheesh!' said Donner. 'You could feed the Spanish Armada with what they have down there.'

'Ho ho ho,' laughed Whitebeard. 'By the noises coming from Blitzen's belly, it may last us a week!'

Blitzen smiled and patted his tummy.

Dasher and Dancer were back next with a huge chest they'd lifted from the cabins. It was so heavy they struggled to carry it, but even Dasher was smiling as it slipped through his arms. Opening it for all to see, it brimmed to the top with twinkling diamonds, sparkling silver pieces and thick bars of gold.

'Merry Christmas!' said Dasher, letting the shining silver pieces run through his hands.

'Here, Donner,' said Dancer, throwing a slab of gold at the cook. 'This'll save you a trip or two to the dentist!'

'Wait, Dancer,' said Whitebeard, 'you know the rules. We'll be getting everything aboard the *Rudolph's Revenge* before we divide the …'

But before he could finish his sentence, the captain caught a glimpse of a glimmering green jewel the size of Blitzen's fist.

'Neptune's noggin!' gasped Whitebeard.

'It's magnificent,' gulped Vixen.

'It's beautiful,' chimed Prancer.

The captain took it from the chest and held the glittering cone up to the moonlight, its shades of green sparkling like the trees of an enchanted forest.

'I've never seen a jewel like it.'

'Nor will you again,' said the Spanish captain, who'd been watching the pirates scornfully. 'You are looking at the Emerald Envy.'

'The Emerald Envy,' repeated Whitebeard in awe. 'Why, it's got to be worth millions! Where did you find such a treasure?'

'We seized it from a wicked witch. A sorcerer no less. It is cursed. You risk a great deal meddling with this treasure.'

'Ho ho ho,' laughed Whitebeard. 'Do you expect me to fall for that? I don't believe in witches, sir, nor magic of any sort. Do you think I'm going to leave this priceless gem here with you just because of a fairy tale?'

'You don't believe me? The witch is our prisoner and is chained below. Ask her yourself. If you dare.'

Whitebeard shot Caganer a sharp look, but before he could reply Cupid returned breathlessly from the hold.

'Captain,' called Cupid, 'this ship's a slaver! There are men chained below.'

Whitebeard stared hard at the Spanish captain now. Caganer shrugged.

'Thank you, Cupid. Bring all below up here to me.'

One by one, those chained below were escorted to the main deck. Bound and shackled, twelve prisoners appeared before Captain Whitebeard. Eleven men and one woman. They had barely a scrap of clothing between them, and all but the woman looked terrified and stood nervously with their heads down. The small old woman just stared straight at Whitebeard with her moss-green eyes.

'Who are these men?' Whitebeard asked the Spanish captain.

'Slaves. We're taking them from Portobelo to Spain. They are evidence for the Grand Inquisitor.'

'Evidence?'

'Yes, evidence that this woman is a witch!'

'And what exactly will they be telling the Grand Inquisitor, señor?'

'That this sorceress turned their children into dolls!'

Whitebeard looked at the strange old lady. He guessed she was about his age, but with her face all cheek and bone, the years had not been kind. Pointy ears poked out from her matted grey hair and her bright-green eyes glared at him. There was no doubting it, she did look a bit witchy.

'I see. And that way she's burned as a witch and Spain keeps this emerald beauty. Is that right?'

'Whatever pleases His Excellency. And she *is* a witch. She foretold that two ships would arrive this night. One foe and one friend. And here you are, our enemy. Very soon our countrymen will be here to save us.'

'You there,' Whitebeard addressed the crone. 'What's your name?'

'My name is Gretchen, Captain,' she squawked.

'Was this emerald yours?'

'Yes, sir.'

'And did you turn these men's children into dolls?'

'I did not, sir.'

Whitebeard paused, stroking his beard. 'Give the men some water, Cupid,' he commanded. 'Vixen, will you translate for me, my dear.'

'Aye, Captain.'

'Look here,' said Whitebeard, addressing the men in chains. 'I'm the pirate Captain Whitebeard and there are those who call me a rascal and a rogue. But I'll never stand for seeing a man or woman held a slave.'

The men looked up at him.

'I can't return your children to you. But I can offer you a new life. Dancer here was once like you. I found him bound in chains. Now, aboard the *Rudolph's Revenge*, he's a free man! If you so wish, you too are free to join us.'

The men looked at each other in shock and disbelief, but each to a man agreed to join the pirate captain.

'Dancer, take them aboard the *Revenge* and get them out of those irons.'

'Aye, Captain.'

As Dancer led the band of shackled men away, the last one turned to the captain with tears in his big brown eyes.

'*Gracias,*' he said with a smile. '*Gracias, señor.*'

The old crone took a step to follow the men.

'Not you, Gretchen,' said Whitebeard, holding up the Emerald Envy. 'I want to know more about this!'

With all eyes on the gem, glimmering in the night sky, no one had noticed a Spaniard hiding behind one of the barrels. Armed with a pistol, he cocked it and took aim at Whitebeard.

BANG!

Now you don't live to be a white-whiskered pirate without a sixth sense for danger; on hearing the click of the flintlock, the captain dived for cover and in doing so dropped the emerald.

The shot missed him completely, but found another target. The bullet hit Prancer in the neck. Screaming, the pirate fell to the ground.

Chapter 7

'Prancer!' cried out Vixen. She rushed to her fallen shipmate who was writhing on the floor in a bloody mess.

In a flash, Dasher went to work and silenced the Spaniard. A swish, a thrust and the sailor was thwarted with a whack on the head.

'Captain, what can we do?' pleaded Vixen as blood oozed from Prancer's neck.

'I can help him,' crowed Gretchen. 'My gem can work its charms. Here, give it to me, sweet girl.'

'Wait!' called out Whitebeard.

'We don't have much time,' urged Gretchen.

Without a second thought, Vixen reached for the fallen jewel.

'No, Vixen,' Whitebeard hollered. 'I said wait!'

But it was too late. Ignoring her captain, Vixen handed the precious stone to the old woman.

'Ancient gem, emerald true,
Show us what your power can do.
Fix this wound with healing glue
And make this man as good as new.'

Glistening in Gretchen's hand, the Emerald Envy shone with the brightness of a thousand stars. The light was so blinding, the pirates had to shield their eyes. Never in their lives had they seen magic before, but sure enough, as the brightness faded, Prancer's wound began to heal.

The crew were silent. All were amazed by this miracle. Prancer's eyes opened, blinking as he rubbed the side of his neck.

'Neptune's noggin!' said Whitebeard, snatching back the emerald as quickly as he could.

'Oh, Prancer,' sniffled Vixen, hugging him as tears rolled down her cheeks.

'WITCH!' yelled the Spanish captain.

'You may well call me witch, but it will do you no good. You and your sorry crew will not live to see another day.'

Captain Caganer was aghast. 'You said two ships would come this night. One friend, one foe.'

'*This* is the friendly ship,' Gretchen cackled, sending a chill down the spine of the Spanish captain. 'Now please, Captain Whitebeard, I have served you a good turn in saving this man's life. Will you not now do the same and let me go, along with what rightfully belongs to me?'

'Not so fast, Gretchen,' said Whitebeard. 'You're coming with us, but this stone is ours now. Think of it as a freedom tax. For we will let you go. Eventually.'

The witch and the captain stared at each other defiantly, while the emerald still glowed.

'Take her aboard the *Rudolph's Revenge*, and make sure you keep her chained,' ordered Whitebeard. 'She's a long way to go yet before we can trust her.'

Helping Prancer to his feet, Vixen alone smiled at Gretchen. The old woman nodded in reply as Blitzen led her to their ship.

'Come,' called Whitebeard. 'If this wretch here is right, there's trouble headed this way.'

Sure enough, not far away, the *Frostbite* sailed closer to the action. The cutthroat crew were drooling like a pack of hungry werewolves. They stared in disbelief at the sight of two ships illuminated by an emerald-green glow. Its brightness was so intense, even from a distance they had to look away.

'Blazin' barnacles!' said Oggin, covering his eyes. 'What on earth is that?'

'Whitebeard,' hissed Frosty.

When the light faded it was as if the ships had disappeared.

'We've lost 'em, Captain,' said Oggin.

'Of course we haven't, Oggin, you fool. They're still there. Ships do not just vanish into thin air. Let your eyes adjust. There, look!'

The captain was right. Keeping their course, the *Frostbite* closed in on our pirates, pistols primed, daggers drawn and marlin spikes at the ready. But before they could launch an attack, the *Rudolph's Revenge* got away. All that was left for the *Frostbite* was the defenceless *Ave Maria*. But with the Spaniard's coffers coughed up already, there was little left for Frosty's crew to strip.

In bargaining for the lives of all aboard his ship, the Spanish captain told Jack Frost everything that had taken place that night. The attack. The emerald. The witch.

'Yes, sir, I'm quite certain,' confirmed Captain Caganer to Frosty. 'And the *Rudolph's Revenge* sailed off in that direction.' He pointed. 'Back towards the Spanish Main. There, Captain, that is all.'

'Thank you, you have been most helpful,' said Frosty slyly. 'Now, Oggin, it's Christmas, is it not?'

'Indeed it is, sir.'

'I rather think it's time to see what my Swiss Army Knives can do.'

'Yes, sir,' agreed Oggin. 'Call out the Switzers!'

The unfortunate Spanish sailors could hear the sound of clashing cutlery long before they saw the menacing shadows appear before them.

'No! Please, Captain. Please!' begged Caganer as the Swiss Guard stepped into the moonlight. 'Please, put away your knives. We have told you everything we know, sir. We have nothing left to give you.'

'There is still one thing you have that I want,' said Frosty, his eyes flashing cruelly. 'You still have your lives!'

Chapter 8

After stashing their loot and making a speedy getaway, the crew aboard the *Rudolph's Revenge* could sit back and enjoy what was left of Christmas Eve.

Slaves no more, the men they'd rescued from the Spanish ship were given fresh clothes as Donner prepared a hearty meal with the stolen stores. Dancer had freed the men with his picklock and had all but one man to go.

'These locks are tricky, friend,' said Dancer with a frown. 'Hang on, I've nearly got it.'

'Thank you,' said the man in irons.

'You speak English?'

'I do.'

'What's your name?'

'They call me Gabriel.'

'I'm Dancer. Nice to meet you.'

Gabriel smiled. 'We have more than doubled the number of your crew.'

'That you have,' replied Dancer. 'We're small, but perfectly formed – what you might call the captain's pick. I was like you, my friend. They were shipping me on a slaver to Hispaniola when the good captain rescued me and some other men destined for a sugar plantation. We were given a choice and I chose to sail on the *Revenge*.'

'And the others?'

'Captain let 'em take the ship and sail for home.'

'You didn't want to go home?'

'I never really had much of a home. My parents died when I was young and my uncle sold me as a slave.'

'That is terrible. Your own family.'

'Aye, well, this is my family now. And it ain't so terrible. No matter what they say about Donner's cooking.'

'Donner?'

'Yes, that's Donner there in the galley kitchen making us dinner. He used to sail with the Barbary pirates until he lost a leg and they left him to rot somewhere near Cuba. The captain saved what's left of his hairy behind and even made him that peg he hobbles around on. Now he's our cook.'

'Who is the girl?'

'That's Vixen. Don't ask me where she's from; she was a gypsy, so everywhere and nowhere really. Couple of years back, Vixen pretended to be a man to sail on a Spanish ship. When they found out she's a girl they marooned her on a desert island. Luckily for her, the captain picked her up and let her sail with us. Now, she's our best sailor.'

'Who's that over there?'

'That funny-looking guy in the blue coat, staring up at nothing with the telescope? That's Comet. He used to be an officer in the Royal Navy. Sometimes I reckon he still thinks he is. They kicked him out for being crazy. Kept saying he'd seen a mermaid.'

'A mermaid?' asked Gabriel.

'Where I'm from, we call them river mummas. Half woman, half fish. I know, mad, ain't it? Anyway, one night, without telling anyone, Comet steers a king's ship off its course and right back to where he'd last seen a mermaid. Of course, he couldn't find her and when his captain found out, they near killed him. They let Comet have another look for the mermaid by draggin' him under their ship with a rope. The barnacles underneath tore him to shreds. He was left to die on a pile of rocks. Lucky for Comet, Captain Whitebeard was not far away to rescue him.'

'What about the others?'

'Dasher, Prancer, Cupid and Blitzen there.' Dancer pointed with his picklock. 'They were all orphaned in the Port Royal earthquake. Ever hear about that? Wiped out thousands of people. Captain took 'em in and near brought 'em up himself. Taught 'em how to sail. How to fight. Pretty much everything they know. Cupid was just a baby at the time. Never knew his parents. Anyway, I guess you could say we're all orphans here, one way or another.'

'Aye, Dancer, that we are,' said Whitebeard, joining the men. 'Donner, when's dinner ready?'

'A minute, Captain, gimme a minute,' he said, dishing out a bowl to Vixen.

'Hey, why's Vixen getting some now?' asked Cupid.

'She's taking food down to our female guest below.'

'No need to torture the old woman,' joked Prancer.

'You've a lot to thank her for,' replied Donner. 'Maybe you should be taking down her food.'

'I don't remember what happened,' said Prancer, scratching his neck.

'Hello, young Vixen,' said Comet as she passed him on her way below.

'Hello, Mister Comet. What are you doing?'

'You know, Vixen. The same thing I do most nights.'

'Looking at the stars?'

'Yes, Vixen, looking at the stars.'

'My mum used to say you can figure a lot out by looking at the stars.'

'Indeed, she's right.'

'She'd be able to tell if we were going to be lucky. Or sad. Or if great challenges lay ahead.'

'Well, I think your mum might have been looking at the stars in a rather different way, my girl. I'm using the stars for navigation. On a clear night, the stars are like a map that can guide us. See there? That's the North Star. It's bright, but far away. That's because we're near the equator. So you see, it shows us where we are and helps us with where we are going.'

'You see that,' said Vixen, pointing to a twinkling constellation. 'That's the Horseshoe, and it means we're *going* to be fine.'

'Ha ha,' laughed Comet. 'I dare say you're right. What have you got there?'

'It's supper for the old lady. You should join the others. Donner's dishing up.'

'Aye, thank you,' said Comet, and Vixen turned to make her way down below.

'Vixen,' called out Comet. 'Be careful with her. She's not to be trifled with.'

'I will,' promised Vixen with a smile. 'I will.'

'It's quite a Christmas Eve for you, friend,' said Prancer to Gabriel. 'First freedom, now a decent feed, and with Donner's cooking you'll be sure to find enough hairs in your bowl to cover that shiny head of yours.'

'Hairs?'

'Aye,' said Prancer. 'Donner's dishes always look like the contents of a barber's bin bag. Look! Worse than picking out fish bones if you ask me.'

'If you don't want it, Prancer, I'll have it,' scoffed Blitzen with his mouth full. The big bear stretched out an enormous paw to snatch the bowl.

'Uh-uh. Calm your farm, Blitzen,' said Prancer, smacking Blitzen's hand away with his spoon.

'Speaking of calm,' said Dasher, picking up a bowl, 'I've never heard anyone lose it like you did when you copped that bullet in the neck. You squealed like a pig.'

The crew laughed. Prancer didn't.

Still fumbling at Gabriel's fetters, Dancer threw down his picklock in frustration.

'It's no use. This just ain't working. Here, Blitzen, come here and gimme a hand.'

Blitzen picked up a nearby hammer and, with one solid swing, smashed the chains to pieces.

'*Gracias*, big man,' said Gabriel.

Blitzen nodded and went back to licking his bowl.

'Is it true?' asked Dancer. 'Did that old lady really turn your children into dolls?'

Gabriel nodded. 'The night the Spanish captured her, she was chained up with us and our little ones. In the morning, all our children were gone. All that was left of them were lifeless dolls.'

Chapter 9

Down below, Vixen held her breath as she made her way to the bilge. Dark and dank, it smelt even worse than Blitzen's armpits on a hot day. Mice and rats jumped and scurried at the sound of footsteps. Nero, the ship's cat, clearly hadn't been doing his job properly. Vixen turned into a room at the very bottom and found Gretchen with her arms chained to the wooden beams.

'This is worse than on the Spanish ship,' she grumbled.

'Well, they had more room,' said Vixen. 'It's a bit of a squeeze upstairs now we have guests.'

'Ah yes, the slaves. I suppose they've been telling lies about me. About how I turned their children into dolls?'

Vixen shrugged, setting down the tray on a barrel.

'And do you believe them?'

Vixen sighed. 'I believe what I see with my own eyes.'

'You're a good girl. I can see that,' whispered the old woman.

Vixen smiled, spooning the old crone a mouthful of Donner's dish. Gretchen spluttered as a hair caught in the back of her throat. Vixen gave her a sympathetic smile and mopped around her mouth.

'You see me chained here, with your own eyes. Do you believe it's fair, to keep me locked up like this?'

'No, I don't …'

'After what I did to save your boyfriend.'

'He's *not* my boyfriend.'

'Yes, but you want him to be.'

There was silence but for the bilge swishing around their ankles.

'The captain says you can't be trusted, and there are those who call you a witch,' Vixen said at last.

'They're not the first to fear my power. And they'll not be the last. Men have always stared at my pointy ears and called me a witch. I have only ever tried to help men, child. I have only ever tried to use my magic to heal. You know that. You've seen that.'

'Aye, there's nothing I can do. I'm sorry.'

'Yet maybe there's something I can do, to prove that I can be trusted?'

'The captain won't let you.'

'I don't mean the captain, girl. I mean you. I see you're not the same as those mean men. You have a kind heart, child. Now, if to you alone I can prove I'm good, you can tell your captain and persuade him to set me free. That is all I ask, to be free like those men above. Those men your good captain saved. I didn't see any of them try to help your pretty pirate when he was shot. But I did, didn't I? And without trying to bargain for his life.'

Vixen gave her another spoonful of stew.

'Listen, child, bring the emerald down here and I will grant you a Christmas wish.'

Vixen winced at first, but lost herself in the moss-green eyes of the old crone.

'I know you like the pretty pirate. The one that I saved. My magic can make him like you too, my dear. I'll help you get what your heart desires, but you must help me. Bring me now my emerald gem, along with your favourite possession in all the world. You're a clever girl, Vixen, and you needn't even risk the emerald in my hand. Just bring it here with your favourite thing and your wish is my command.'

Now, is Vixen the sort of lass to be tempted by such a proposal? Of course she's not! Vixen's made of stronger stuff and she's got more sense than to go trusting mysterious old crones with obvious designs on freedom. No, Prancer would like her for who she was or not at all. She'd *never* try to trick him with magic. Vixen smiled politely, thanked Gretchen for the kind offer and made her way back upstairs to join the crew.

'Ho ho ho,' laughed Whitebeard. 'My sailing friends, my thieves. First, I would like to congratulate everyone here. It was a brave effort tonight and you all did a first-class job. Now, we are to divide the spoils! It's time for your fair share. Diamonds, gold, sapphires, rubies; there's plenty of silverware!'

'I'd say you owe Vixen your share, Prancer,' sniped Dasher. 'Although she probably wouldn't accept it. Ha! The way she rushed to your rescue. True love, I'd say.'

The crew laughed.

'Shut your trap, Dasher. Or I'll shut it for you,' threatened Prancer.

'Bit tetchy aren't we, Prancer? Probably a bit lovesick because Vixen's been down below with that old wretch for so long you miss her!'

'Take it back, Dasher!'

'I will not. You're in love. It's obvious!'

'I do not love, Vixen. She's … why, she's a pirate! I can't be in love with a pirate. No matter how much she might like me.'

All eyes and ears were on Prancer and no one noticed Vixen back on deck, approaching the gang.

'I want a nice girly girl. You know, a lass who dresses nice, with blonde curls and … at least fifty thousand in the bank.'

The crew laughed again as Vixen drew closer.

'I don't want some leather-skinned gypsy with nothing but scars and rope burns to her name.'

The raucous laughter of the crew abruptly stopped when they caught the look on Vixen's heartbroken face.

Chapter 10

Turning her back on her shipmates, tears streaming down her face, Vixen ran below.

Prancer took a step to go after her.

'Leave her,' said Whitebeard. 'Leave her be.'

Prancer turned back to Dasher and smacked him hard in the face. Dasher launched himself forward to bring Prancer crashing to the deck and the pair began pummelling each other with their fists.

BANG!

Whitebeard fired a pistol in the air. It was enough to shock the brawling pirates who stopped still and faced their captain.

'That's enough, you two.'

Blitzen picked them both up by the scruff of the neck.

'That's not how we do things on my ship. You know the rules. If you want to fight each other, fetch the Stoomps.'

Dasher and Prancer stared at each other.

'Well,' said Whitebeard, 'what's it to be?'

Prancer wiped a trickle of blood from his lip. 'Bring out the Stoomps,' he said.

'You're mad,' said Cupid. 'Dasher will thrash you.'

Whitebeard looked at Prancer. 'The loser will part with half their plunder,' he warned.

'You heard me,' said Prancer.

'Very well. Mister Comet, the Stoomps, if you please.'

Comet nodded and headed for the captain's cabin.

'What's going on?' Gabriel asked Dancer.

'Disputes between us are settled with Stoompfloggen sticks,' said Dancer. 'If anyone wishes to settle a score with a shipmate, the captain sends for the Stoomps.'

'Stoompfloggen?' asked Gabriel. 'Is that even a thing?'

'It is aboard the *Rudolph's Revenge*,' said Dancer.

'What are the rules?'

'It's quite simple,' explained Dancer. 'It's a lot like a duel. A large circle is drawn with chalk on the deck. Or in the sand if we're ashore. Then the two opponents enter the circle, each with a Stoomp.'

'That's a cutlass-shaped stick made out of wood,' interrupted Cupid.

'Right you are,' continued Dancer. 'The aim is to strike your opponent above the ankle or below the knee.'

'Before you start, you have to cross Stoomps three times and say "En garde",' Cupid jumped in again.

'Who's explaining this, Cupid? You or me?'

'You are Dancer. Sorry.'

'Anyway, there's no time limit and it's the best of three. The loser must back down and pay up his plunder.'

'Seems straightforward enough,' said Gabriel.

'Aye, it is.'

Comet returned with two cutlass-shaped sticks.

'For those new to our crew,' said Whitebeard sternly, 'let this be a lesson to you. Cupid, draw me a ring, lad.'

'Aye, Captain.'

Cupid took a stick of chalk and marked out a large circle and in stepped Dasher and Prancer.

'Right, you both know the rules. If you're struck above the ankle, you lose. If you're struck below the knee, you lose. If you step outside the circle, you lose.'

Below deck, Vixen rummaged through her sea chest and pulled out a bunch of pressed mistletoe. A trinket from her gypsy days.

'No, Vixen!' I hear you cry. 'You're better than this!'

And she was too. But our girl was upset and angry and thought she knew a way to prove them all wrong.

'I'll show them,' she muttered under her breath as she left for the captain's cabin.

In the circle, Dasher and Prancer faced one another.

Clank … Clank … Clank …

'En garde,' said Dasher.

'En garde,' said Prancer.

And they were off.

Dasher's sideways stance was textbook. Right arm forward, with left hand casually at his hip. Prancer looked a lot less classy. He kept the tip of his Stoomp pointed to the ground, offering solid protection to Dasher's nifty twirls and thrusts.

Dasher had his man on the back foot and it was defence all the way for Prancer who desperately tried to block each of Dasher's advances …

Speaking of advances, where was Vixen? Oh yes, she was in the captain's cabin and had picked the lock to his safe, the naughty possum.

'It'll only be a minute, Nero,' she said to the black cat, who from the comfort of a cushion on the captain's chair watched on with a worried look.

'Stop looking at me like that, Nero!'

And Vixen was off, racing through the dimly lit corridors below and back to the bilge.

Thwack, thwack, thwack. The duel continued. Dasher had to hand it to Prancer, he was giving him a run for his money. But we all know 'The Blade' was just playing with Prancer; with a nifty sidestep and a thrust, Dasher struck his opponent's shin. Boy, it hurt.

'One nil to Dasher,' said Whitebeard.

Cheers all round.

Back below, Vixen held up both her mistletoe and the Emerald Envy. The gem was glowing almost as much as Gretchen's bright-green eyes.

'Is this really your most precious thing?' asked the old crone, looking at the string of berries.

'Yes,' said Vixen.

'Are you sure? No gold or silver? Not even a brass buckle?'

'No. This mistletoe was the last thing my mother gave me before she died. It's the only thing I have left from home.'

'Very well, my dear, I'll see what I can do.'

Back on deck and it was round two.

Clank … Clank … Clank …

'En garde!'

Prancer's shin was throbbing, but he was not going to just stand there and defend as Dasher made him look stupid. This time Prancer was on the attack. While he might not have been as stylish as Dasher, the lad could move all right. A few more swings and he might just land one …

'Hear me now, stone and stem.
Let love flower in this root.
Passion fill the berries white.
Let desire be your fruit.
Mistletoe enchanted;
blooms your loving chance.
Hold it high above your lips
and you'll kiss your sweet romance.'

The emerald glowed green, the snow-white berries on the mistletoe shone brightly like glimmering pearls and Vixen's face beamed with joy as she smiled at her new friend.

Thwack, thwack, thwack. Prancer and Dasher fought on. Prancer moved swiftly and, with an athletic display that was quite unexpected, managed to get behind Dasher and hit him hard on the back of his calf.

'Owww!' cried Dasher.

'Now who sounds like a squealing pig?' quipped Prancer, getting to his feet.

'That's not fair,' said Dasher, looking towards the captain.

'One all,' said Whitebeard.

'Thank you so much, Gretchen! Will it really work?'

'Indeed it will, my sweet. Indeed it will.'

Prancer and Dasher both straightened up ahead of round three. There was everything to play for.

'Ha! Not as hot as you think you are, are you, Dasher?' goaded Prancer.

'Don't think you can pull a move like that again, you cheat. You got lucky.'

Each dripping with sweat, they raised their Stoomps for the decider.

Dasher's eyes narrowed. Prancer's opened wide.

Clank … Clank …

BOOM!

Before the pirates could even mark the final round, cannon fire lit up the night sky as cannonballs tore with ferocious force into the starboard side of the *Rudolph's Revenge.* The panicked pirates dropped to the ground in terror; they had just copped a broadside from Frosty and his fiendish crew.

Chapter 11

Below deck, the attack threw Vixen to the floor and both the enchanted mistletoe and the Emerald Envy fell from her hands and tumbled within Gretchen's reach. The crone picked up her gem and cackled menacingly.

'Fool!' she laughed as the glowing emerald melted away her chains. Vixen instantly recognised the old woman for the cheat she was.

No longer bound, Gretchen held the emerald high over her head. A ray of shining green light flowed down like a shower, transforming the wicked creature from a crone to a wrinkle-free elven beauty.

Beside herself with anger and fear, Vixen pulled a dagger from her belt and threw it at her betrayer. But Gretchen was too fast and, waving the emerald like a wand, caught the blade mid-air and turned it on Vixen. The knife flew at the pirate, catching her coat and pinning her to the timber behind.

'Not so fast, my dear,' crowed Gretchen.

'You horrid creature. I trusted you!' Vixen spat at the floor. 'Now it's clear you really are an evil witch who turns children into lifeless dolls!'

'I'm no witch, my dear. I'm an ancient elf and I promise you I do not waste my time turning children into dolls.'

'Then … why? Why have you turned on me? I thought we were friends.'

'Friends. Ha! Your loyalties are with your captain, child, and he would never have released me with this stone. It is too powerful. This is an elven emerald, crafted by my kin as a promised gift to a newborn king. The jealous King Herod stole it from us on our way to Bethlehem, and ever since, the power of envy has seeded in this gem. Oh yes, it's a feast for the eyes, but a famine for the soul. Once jewelled in mad King Herod's crown, such was his envy, he went from town to town, killing in his rage as he tried to find the infant child who made him so jealous. Since then, this stone has cursed all men. A touch is enough to topple kingdom, crown and throne.'

'If it is so dangerous, what do you want with it?'

'Man is not fit to touch it,' said Gretchen. 'It belongs to my people. I will use it to take my rightful position as Queen of the Elves.'

Another cannonball smashed into the side of the ship and Gretchen decided it was time to leave.

'I must go, child, thank you for bringing me what's mine.'

The elven witch laughed a terrible laugh as she held up the glowing emerald, blinding Vixen. She waved it once more and conjured a spider's web of green lace to trap the pirate firmly against the wall. When Vixen opened her eyes, Gretchen was gone.

The fight below was over, but above deck it raged on. Well within range, the *Frostbite* fired volley after volley at the *Rudolph's Revenge*. Flaming cannonballs filled the sky and rained down upon Whitebeard's ship. Smoke and splinters stung the eyes and skin of the crew, who were desperately trying to fight back.

Donner, Blitzen and the powder monkeys were hard at it on the cannon, and even Dasher and Prancer had put aside their differences to wage war against the overpowering galleon.

'Come on, lads, don't give in!' cried out Whitebeard. 'Ready. Aim. Fire!'

A round of cannonballs flew towards the *Frostbite*. Two fell short. One tore through a sail as the last round grazed Frosty's quarterdeck. The *Frostbite* crew laughed at Whitebeard's attempt to fightback and our pirates' hearts sank.

'It's no use,' said Dasher. 'They are too big, too strong and too far away.'

Another round smashed into the *Rudolph's Revenge*, hitting the top sail which crashed down onto half the men Whitebeard saved from the slaver. Cries for help and groans of pain added to the inescapable roar of battle.

In the chaos no one saw Gretchen emerge from below, but the elven witch quickly caught sight of Whitebeard. She lifted the emerald high above her head to conjure all the power she could to strike at her foe. The blinding light caught Whitebeard's attention and, sensing he was about to be struck, he pulled a pistol from his belt. But it was too late; Gretchen had already started unleashing her spell. Then a blast from Frosty smashed into the deck and Gretchen was knocked off her feet. The emerald flew through the air and the almighty ball of bright-green flame meant for Whitebeard soared across the sea to the *Frostbite*. A crash of thundering light engulfed Frosty's vessel, to cheers from our pirates.

The Emerald Envy tumbled to the side of the *Rudolph's Revenge*. Both Whitebeard and

Gretchen raced each other to the glowing treasure. It was neck and neck as they leapt for it. Colliding, the opponents crashed into each other so hard that Whitebeard sent Gretchen into the side of the ship and the jewel flying into the unforgiving arms of the ocean.

'Noooo!' Gretchen cried, as the emerald sank beneath the waves and she was transformed back into the body of an old crone.

But if you think that was bad for Gretchen, it was nothing compared to the knock on the head she received from Blitzen.

Chapter 12

To the stern of our ship now. Oh yes, stern indeed. Seated behind his table in the captain's cabin, Whitebeard frowned as Vixen told him most of what had happened that night. Tears rolled down her cheeks as she stared at the floor; she couldn't bear to look up and see the disappointment on his fuzzy face.

'Vixen, please tell me. Why did you risk our ship and all aboard by meddling with that witch? The *Rudolph's Revenge* is in pieces, half our new shipmates are injured and we've lost a priceless treasure. Well, you're lucky that we're still alive.'

Vixen stayed silent. She didn't know what to say. She couldn't tell him about Prancer, the mistletoe and the love spell. She tried looking up and into her captain's searching blue eyes but couldn't.

'Vixen, my girl, I can't tell you how much you've impressed us all since joining our crew. There's no one faster up the shroud or quicker with a knot. You're the best sailor we have. But you do worry me sometimes. What am I to do with you?'

'I'm sorry, Captain,' said Vixen as a pool of tears puddled on the cabin floor. 'I'm so sorry.'

'There, there, my girl. What are you trying to do now? Drown us?'

Vixen laughed through her tears and two large green balls of snot shot from her nostrils like bunged-up seaweed. Whitebeard passed her a hanky and poured them both a drink.

'Here, get this down you and you'll be fit for a flogging.'

Vixen looked up sharply.

'No,' said Whitebeard reassuringly, 'there'll be no flogging for you, my girl. We don't do that sort of thing on the *Rudolph's Revenge*. Besides, old Frosty was on to us anyway and if you hadn't handed the witch that emerald, we'd all have been blown to kingdom come. As I say, it's luck that saved us. In any case, you were tricked by that wicked elf's witchcraft. Plain and simple. We can all see that. The sooner we're rid of this so-called Elf Queen, the better.'

'Thank you, Captain.'

'And you say that the Emerald Envy was made by elves for the very first Christmas?'

Vixen nodded, taking another sip. 'That's what she told me.'

'What I don't understand is how she got you to bring her the emerald. Unless,' he mused, 'unless you craved magic yourself. It wouldn't, by any chance, have anything to do with a handsome young pirate we both know?'

Vixen froze.

'What did you want? Revenge? A kiss?' Whitebeard's voice became softer. 'Love?'

Vixen burst into tears and Whitebeard could barely console her.

'There, there,' he said. 'There's no need for tears. Please don't cry. Here, how about I cheer you up with a nice sea shanty? I've been working on just the one for this sort of thing.'

'No thank you, Captain,' said Vixen, who threatened with a song, had no trouble pulling herself together. She'd heard the captain's sea shanties before and they were usually a terrible assault on the eardrums. What the captain lacked in talent, he made up for in volume.

But Captain Whitebeard was undeterred and cleared his throat. Well, at least he wasn't going to play his squeeze box as well. That really would feel like punishment.

'Hang on a tick, Vixen. This always sounds better with my concertina,' said Whitebeard as he rummaged around under the desk for his musical instrument. 'Here we are!'

Nero let out a screech in protest as the captain began playing the first strangled chords. Vixen took a deep breath.

'We're all like little ships, my dear.
Each bobbing on the tide.
In navigating this sea called life,
We rock from side to side.
Your head might steer you well enough,
But it's your heart that gets you there.
Like the sails, it opens up to catch
wind rushing through the air.

Heave-to, my little deario,
Turn and face the gale.
Master your sails, head held high,
And you'll find that you prevail.
Look to catch the wind, my dear;
North, South, East or West.
Look after your sails and you'll survive,
Stormy squall or fierce tempest.

Heave-to, my little deario;
Relax and take a break.
It's the best way to survive at sea
When your hearty sails all ache ...'

'Thank you, Captain,' interrupted Vixen. 'That's cheered me up already.'

'That's just the first bit, there's plenty more,' insisted Whitebeard, taking a deep breath to begin again.

'It's very … unique,' said Vixen, cutting him off. 'You have a … *rare* talent.'

'Why, thank you,' said Whitebeard merrily, putting down his instrument with satisfaction.

Vixen sighed with relief and looked at her captain. 'You sing of aching sails, but what can you know of heartache?'

'My dear Vixen. It never ceases to amaze me how young people forget that we old sailors were young once too. You may not believe me, my dear, but love once brushed my cheek. Aye, a lovelier lass you'd never meet than my dear, sweet Mary.'

Getting up, Whitebeard stoked the dying fire. Gazing into the dancing embers, he found himself rekindling memories of long ago. Vixen had never seen her captain with such a mist in his clear blue eyes.

'Aye. I suppose we were a little younger than you are now when we first met. Long ago, when I was just a poor orphan boy growing up on the streets of old London town. Nasty place it was back then for a street urchin. Dozens of us living in squalor and all we had to eat was porridge. Well, I say porridge. It tasted more like sawdust and watery rat's milk. The only time we ever ate anything better was on a Sunday morning when a kind baker from Pudding Lane rolled up on his horse and cart to hand out loaves of freshly baked bread. By the stars, I can smell it now.

'One autumn day the baker brought along his daughter to help him and, as usual, the street urchins swept in like seagulls to snatch the bread. There were the usual fights over every last scrap. Me? I just stood there looking at the most beautiful face I'd ever seen. Lovely Mary. Wrapped up like Little Red Riding Hood in her bright red coat. She even smiled back at me and for the first time in my life I felt like I had something to live for. Aye, crumbs of hope she fed me that day.

'From then on I longed for Sundays to catch sight of her and after a while we got to know each other and fell in love. But I wasn't the only one to take a shine to young Mary. Oh no, there was another. Jack Frost, no less. Aye, he and I grew up on the streets together and you'd even have called us friends. Well, that was until Mary came along. You see, Jack got jealous of me and Mary. It consumed him.

'One night when we were making bread together at her bakery, jealous Jack locked us inside and started a fire. Trapped in that fiery hell, I did all I could to save her from the flames, but the blaze was too hot and the flames too high. I couldn't get to her, and my dearest Mary, my lovely one, I never saw again.'

Whitebeard wiped a tear from his rosy red cheek and looked up at Vixen.

'The fire swept through the whole city. The Great Fire of London they call it now. Burned for almost a week. From that moment on, Frosty and I became sworn enemies and we've fought each other ever since. So you see, young

Vixen, when it comes to sails, I once caught a breeze, just like you. And still I sail with Mary in my heart.'

Vixen couldn't help but feel sad for her captain and gave the old man a hug.

'Right, young Vixen, be off with you. It's time for bed. Merry Christmas, my dear, and I promise, in the morning she'll be right.'

Chapter 13

In his career as a pirate, Oggin had found himself in some frightful situations. There was the terrible time he'd had a tooth removed by a rum-soaked surgeon wielding nothing but a corkscrew. Then there was the horrible moment he thought he'd bleed to death after being run through by a corsair's cutlass. But in all his years at sea, there was no task more terrifying than knocking on the door of Jack Frost's cabin when the captain was in a foul mood. Fellow shipmates had been known to enter and never return …

Oggin tapped timidly at the door.

'Enter,' came the cruel voice from within.

The door creaked open and Oggin stepped inside. It was dark but for the silvery touch of moonlight illuminating the gothic furnishings and menacing skulls that decorated the coffin-like cabin. His back to Oggin, Jack Frost sat in a high-backed chair looking out to sea. The captain's long fingers were arched in a steeple beneath his thin lips as he schemed.

'Well, Oggin, don't just stand there gaping. What have you to report?'

'The fire is out, sir,' said Oggin, trembling.

'Very well. It took you long enough. There is damage?'

'We've lost our mainsail, sir, much of the deck has been reduced to charcoal and many of the men have been barbecued pretty bad by the blaze. I've not seen burns on 'em this bad since we spent that week on Antigua and forgot the sunscreen.'

'Have we lost the *Rudolph's Revenge*?'

'We have.'

Jack Frost was white hot with rage. A seething, jealous rage. For if what the Spanish captain said was true, Whitebeard had managed to get his porky little hands on a powerful emerald capable of all sorts of devilish destruction. That kind of thing is like blood to a vampire for terrible villains like old Frosty. The Emerald Envy was something he wanted very much and he'd stop at nothing to get it.

Jack Frost leaned around the back of his chair to look directly at Oggin. 'Now look here, you squalid little squonk, we're going to catch up with that hairy hound, we're going to find a way to get our hands on this so-called Emerald Envy and we're going to destroy Whitebeard. If we don't, Oggin, you know who I'm going to blame, don't you?'

Oggin gulped and looked at his feet to escape the cyclops stare. 'Me, sir?'

'Yes, Oggin. You.'

Little did Jack Frost know, Captain Whitebeard had lost the precious stone and was now sound asleep in the comfort of his cosy cabin.

All was peace aboard the *Rudolph's Revenge*. The silence was interrupted only by the pirates' snores and the faint sound of the waves gently rocking the ship like a baby in a cradle.

At midnight the distant chime of bells rang to announce it was Christmas Day. It was enough to startle the captain and his eyes opened wide. Something wasn't right.

Sitting up, Whitebeard got the fright of his life. For there at the foot of the bed stood a girl wearing a hooded red coat.

'Neptune's noggin!' he cried. 'Mary!'

The vision pulled back her hood, smiled and nodded at the captain.

'Is that really you? What are you doing here?' he asked.

Putting a finger to her lips, the girl turned, opened the cabin window and before he could say another word she leapt out of sight.

'No, Mary!' shouted Whitebeard, throwing off the bed sheets and rushing to the ledge. Looking out of the window he expected to see the girl being swept out to sea, but to his amazement the ocean had vanished. Instead of the dark waters of the Caribbean, there was a blanket of white snow. The captain rubbed his eyes, turning back to his cabin to get a grip on reality. Shaking his head, he looked back outside and ducked as a snowball flew past his head and hit the timber panels behind him. From below Mary laughed, rolling up another ball of snow.

'Come, Nicholas,' she said and gestured for the old sea captain to jump down.

Whitebeard pulled on his red coat and looked down in disbelief. Was he really going to jump?

Taking a deep breath, he leapt out into the night sky and landed on a cushion of marshmallow snow. Strangely, his old aching bones no longer felt weary and his big red coat felt a good deal roomier than usual. Somehow his hands were lost in his long red cuffs and he struggled to wrestle them out from the sleeves.

When he saw his hands, he gasped. No longer old and wrinkled, they were small and soft. He held them up to his face and got an even bigger shock. For the first time in years, he could feel the smoothness of his cheeks. His white beard was gone.

'What is happening, Mary?'

'Do you remember when we were young, Nicholas?'

'I do.'

'Do you remember what we loved doing most?'

'Skating,' he said.

'Here,' she said, handing young Nicholas a gold box wrapped in a colourful red bow. 'Merry Christmas.'

Opening the gift, he was overjoyed to find a pair of brand-new ice skates.

'Thank you, Mary,' he said and without a second thought, pulled them on and laced them up.

'Come,' she said, and off they skated on the mirror of frozen ice.

Holding hands beneath the stars, they skated side by side as snowflakes fell softly from the skies above.

Turning, twisting and gliding, Nicholas felt a happiness in his heart he had long forgotten.

'Mary, is this just a dream?'

'Yes,' she said. 'You must enjoy it, Nicholas. This is the last time you will ever get to sleep or dream on Christmas Eve.'

'What do you mean?' he asked, skating to a halt.

Mary turned back to face him and held his hands as the snow began to fall thick and fast around them.

'It is time for you to change your ways, Nicholas. It is time for you to stop taking from people and give back.'

'Give back?'

Her hazel eyes stared hard at him as she held his hands tight. 'You must rediscover your kindness, Nicholas. If you do not, mankind is in great danger.'

'Rediscover my kindness? No more sleep on Christmas Eve? This doesn't make sense, Mary ...'

'You have been chosen, Nicholas.'

'Whatever do you mean? Chosen for what?'

'Chosen to save Christmas. There are those who would steal the magic of Christmas and use it for their own wicked ends. You are the one to stop them.'

Letting go of his hands, Mary turned and skated away.

'What? I don't understand. Stop who?' cried Nicholas, skating after her.

'You know who,' called Mary. In the gathering snow storm she began to disappear from sight.

'You must stop him, Nicholas. You can do it.'

'Mary! Come back. Mary! Where are you?'

Nicholas saw a flicker of red in the wall of snow and ice ahead.

'Mary, wait! What am I to do?'

'Stay true to yourself, your *real* self and you will prevail. I will send a special friend to help you. You will know him as my envoy, for on his chest he'll wear my coat.'

'Wait, Mary!'

Lost in the blinding force of the blizzard, Mary was gone.

Nicholas tried to open his eyes, but the icy wind and snow stung his face like a swarm of wasps. Squinting, he looked up and came face to face with the terrifying image of Jack Frost. Shocked by the wicked villain, Nicholas fell backwards towards the cold, hard bed of snow …

Chapter 14

Shaken from his sleep, Whitebeard jerked awake. His old bones creaked like the timber of his ship. The vivid images from his dream swirled in his head, shining as brightly as the sunlight spilling into his cabin.

Before he could gather himself, there was a knock at the door. Startled, Whitebeard jumped at the sound.

'Merry Christmas, Captain!' said Cupid, bounding in with breakfast. 'Here you are, Spain's finest.'

'Merry Christmas, Cupid. Thank you.'

Cupid left the captain to his breakfast. The tray was filled with everything he could have wished for: coffee, cream, ham and eggs. Buttered toast and marmalade. But the captain was off his food. Instead, he sat stunned until he heard a strange *rat-a-tat-tatting* at his window.

Curious, he inched closer to the pane and there, pecking at the glass, he saw a cheeky robin redbreast.

'What have we here? What are you doing here, so far from winter's snow?'

Whitebeard opened the window to welcome in the little visitor.

Cautiously, the robin peeped in his head, considering the captain carefully. Whitebeard smiled at the bird and offered him a crumb.

'I wonder,' he puzzled. 'Perhaps we share a friend who also wears a coat of red?'

The robin paused, cocking his head to one side before taking another step.

'Easy now,' Whitebeard reassured his new friend and nudged the crumb a little closer. 'Don't worry, no one here is going to hurt you.'

He spoke too soon, for Nero the cat was crouching behind a pillow, ready to pounce.

With a wiggle of his bottom, the cat leapt in the air, claws extended.

'No, Nero!' shouted Whitebeard, sending his breakfast tray flying. Coffee, ham and eggs splattered on the wood-panelled walls and the tray crashed down as he desperately tried to defend the little bird. But the cat was too quick and had seized the redbreast. Terrified, the bird fought to wrestle his head out of the cat's mouth.

'Drop him now, Nero! This instant!' Whitebeard demanded.

The mischievous moggy looked hurt, but spat the bird out. Whitebeard picked up the robin as the door to the cabin swung open.

'Everything okay, Captain?' asked Cupid, looking around at the sorry mess and seeing the bird. 'Did you get something from Donner's beard stuck in your throat?'

'No, no, Cupid, I'm quite all right,' sighed Whitebeard, gently stroking the robin's feathered breast to calm him.

'Beggin' your pardon, Captain, but the crew were wondering if there's a planking to begin?'

'Ah yes. But here, I want you to meet my new friend.'

Recovered from his shock, the little robin chirped his way onto the captain's shoulder.

'What's his name?' asked Cupid, offering the redbreast a tiny crumb.

'I suppose his name is Robin,' replied the captain.

Out on deck there was a buzz of excitement. Not only was it Christmas, but the pirates were looking forward to making Gretchen walk the plank. The crew waited expectantly while Dancer and Blitzen fetched her from the bilge.

All morning Vixen had done all she could to avoid Prancer. When he was down below, she helped Donner in the galley. When he came up, she'd head downstairs to check on the injured crew. Now, as the shipmates gathered, she skulked at the back, but Prancer spotted her and walked over.

'Vixen, about what I said last night … I didn't …'

'You don't have to say anything.'

'I just … well. Here.' Prancer held out a fancy pair of embroidered gauntlet gloves. 'Merry Christmas.'

Vixen smiled, risking a glance at the young man.

'They're lambskin, I think. Pinched them from one of the señoritas last night. We can always tar 'em if you want to make 'em … more practical.'

Blushing, Vixen didn't know what to say. 'Thank you Prancer,' she said with a smile. 'I'm afraid I didn't get you anything.'

'You saved my life last night, Vixen. What more could anyone ask for? Come on, we should join the others.'

Joining the gang, most of the other pirates wished Prancer and Vixen a merry Christmas.

'Here they are,' said Dasher. 'The happy couple. You won't be so happy when I lift half your plunder from you later, Prancer.'

'There will be no playing for plunder today,' announced Whitebeard, stepping out on deck. 'Ho ho ho! Merry Christmas, one and all!' he said with Robin perched happily on his shoulder. 'I trust we are all well this morning? Gabriel, how are your fellows today?'

'Thank you, Captain. They're on the mend. We're taking good care of them.' Gabriel's smile disappeared as Gretchen was lead out onto the main deck. The elven creature scowled at the awaiting crew. Gabriel stared daggers at the woman and the reception she received from the rest of the pirates wasn't much warmer.

'The plank, the plank, the plank,' they cried.

Defiant, Gretchen met their gaze and laughed. 'Fools! Has it occurred to you that by making me walk the plank, you'll reunite me with my emerald? Then I will be back to haunt you. Look at you all. Here I am before you in chains and yet you are still scared of me. And after what I did to save you. To save all of you. None of you would be here this minute if it wasn't for me. All I ever wanted is what's rightfully mine.'

The crew cheered and jeered.

'All right, my friends, that's enough,' boomed Whitebeard over the cries. 'There's to be no planking. We'll be saying farewell to Gretchen here, in a rather different way.'

'Will we be blasting her out of a gun?' asked Blitzen.

'I'd love to see how far she went,' said Donner.

'Go on, it'd be so much fun!' called Cupid.

'No, my friends. It's Christmas Day and I want us to find an island where we can repair our ship and rest. Then, when we're done, we'll maroon the she-devil.'

Before long, Cupid had scouted a small desert island. For most of the crew it felt good to be weighing anchor for the first time in weeks. Repairs to the top mast were made in no time at all and the pirates prepared for a beach party.

Prancer and Vixen helped Donner with the supplies for a barbecue as Dasher and Dancer headed to the bilge to fetch their prisoner.

'No planking, no playing for plunder,' remarked Dasher. 'He's going soft, I tell you.'

'It's Christmas, man,' said Dancer. 'Will you quit your whingeing for just one day?'

The pirates escorted the miserable wretch to the shore.

'Welcome to your new home,' said Dasher. 'Elf Isle!'

There wasn't much to the island and the pirates walked Gretchen to a cluster of palm trees rooted in a clear dusting of white sand. As ever, the elf was full of venom as the pirates chained her to a tree trunk.

'You fools, you will live to regret this. I will make you all pay for leaving me here. You will suffer for the rest of your lives.'

'Look here, witch,' warned Dasher. 'We don't have to settle you in the shade. Give it a rest or we'll tie you to that rock over there and you'll bake in the noonday sun.'

Before you could say 'Donner's kebabs', the ship's cook had knocked up a delicious barbecue. The shipmates wolfed down their food and after they'd licked the last bone clean, their bellies made sweet gurgling sounds as they lazed happily in the sunshine.

'Captain,' said Gabriel, 'it's so long since we've been free to dive in the ocean and wade into water without shackles around our ankles. Can we go for a swim?'

''Course you can, me lad,' said Whitebeard, mid snooze. 'You don't have to ask me.'

'You shouldn't go swimming so soon after eating,' cautioned Dancer.

'Says who?' laughed Cupid, who was already half stripped and running to the shore.

This looked too good to Gabriel and his mates and they raced each other to the open arms of the ocean. The men sprinted past Cupid and jumped in to the clear blue water with a refreshing splash.

'You know what?' said Dancer, turning to his shipmates. 'They're right.'

Laughing in agreement, the crew darted to join the others. In the clear shallow waters of the Caribbean, the shipmates saw a kaleidoscope of colour. Angelfish and parrotfish. Butterflyfish and frogfish. Squirrelfish and smooth trunkfish. All the colours of the rainbow glided together in harmony.

Blitzen catapulted Cupid into the air and he splashed with joy. Prancer pulled playfully at Vixen's feet to drag her under and serve her with a mouthful of salt water. Dasher and Dancer practised handstands as Donner and Whitebeard gave their beards a nice scrub. Comet didn't take his eyes off the marine life below.

Then all of a sudden … there was a cry of surprise and delight:

'Mermaid!'

Chapter 15

Comet's head twitched as he almost choked to death on the water he'd swallowed.

'Mm … mm … mermaid!' he sang out again.

'I don't see anything,' said Vixen.

'Comet's been swigging the salt water again,' said Dasher.

'No I haven't,' insisted Comet. 'Look! There!'

'That's enough, Comet,' said Whitebeard. 'You know I think you're a fine sailor and an excellent navigator, but you're as mad as a March hare if you think you've seen an ocean nymph!'

'Look, Captain!' Cupid pointed to the clear blue water beneath them. 'He's right!'

And sure enough, a beautiful mermaid swam towards the radiant sunshine and popped up beside Whitebeard.

'Sink me!' he declared.

Half-fish, half-girl, the sea maiden was a picture. Her long green hair was as shiny as seaweed; her snow-white face as pretty as any angel he might imagine, but with sandy specks freckling her nose and fiery red eyes melting his gaze. He didn't know where to look but down at the large purple tail flexing in the water below.

'Wait! There's more than one, there's two,' announced Vixen.

'There's a few more than that,' said Prancer. 'Look!'

As the pirates tried to count the mermaids, they soon discovered they were surrounded by dozens of the sea creatures. Each of the maidens looked alike, but where some had shiny green hair with purple tails, others were orange and blue.

Just as our pirates began to grow uneasy with the mermaids circling them, the maidens began

to sing in harmony. Their sweet voices sounded unlike anything the crew had ever heard; as the music touched each of their souls, the pirates were moved to tears.

'It's so … so beautiful,' said Blitzen, tears rolling down his face and into the sea.

'You were right, Comet!' admitted Prancer, wiping his cheeks.

Whitebeard simply stared at the majesty of the mermaids and smiled as their song filled his heart.

As the pirates listened to the mermaids' music, it became clear their melody contained a message:

You who live on floating trees,
We call wind-catchers of the seas.
We'd never wish to appear to you,
But we need your help, oh help us do!
Our young were snatched by evil trolls,
Who plan to make them sushi rolls.
We can't help them, for they're on the land,
So we need you, who walk on sand.

Sail on and enter their fearsome fort,
Save them, please, and don't get caught!
Once the trolls are overthrown,
We'll return to you this emerald stone!

Before the pirates' astonished eyes, the mermaid next to Whitebeard held up the Emerald Envy, shining in all its glory.

Our dolphin friends will be your guide,
To the Isle of Gula where the trolls hide.
Release our young into the sea,
And we'll give you back this green trophy.
We know you want the gem you lost,
An act of kindness its only cost.

'Captain,' said Gabriel, 'if the trolls have the mermaids' young, maybe they have our children too?'

'Jumping jellyfish! You're right,' said Whitebeard. 'Maiden fair, did these trolls you speak of leave anything in place of your young?'

The mermaids held up three lifeless dolls. They looked terrifying and not the sort of thing you'd give a child as a present.

'They're the same!' shouted Gabriel, and he and the other fathers began speaking rapidly in Spanish.

Whitebeard looked at the men and his crew, then turned back to the mermaids.

'Gracious maidens of the sea, we understand your plight. Please allow me to talk with my crew before we accept your quest.'

'I'm not sure about this,' cautioned Dasher.

'You know I hate agreeing with *him*,' said Prancer, 'but should we be risking our lives? I mean, what do we really have to gain? We already have stacks of loot and no offence to our new shipmates, but their children are probably already, you know … '

'Come on, you two,' said Vixen. 'We have to at least try.'

'I'm with you, Vixen,' agreed Dancer.

'Thank you,' said Gabriel.

'Well, Captain,' asked Comet, 'what do you think?'

Whitebeard smiled at his crew. 'My thieves, my sailors, my friends. What we must do now is as clear to me as the water that surrounds this island. We must rescue the children from the trolls. Yes, there may be danger. Yes, we risk a great deal. But think of what we have to gain. The Emerald Envy alone spells an end to us risking our necks for plunder. We need never pirate again.'

'I like being a pirate,' said Blitzen.

'Long may you continue. If you wish. I've pirated for long enough. It's time for me to hang up my sword. All I ask of you is one last adventure together.'

From the shadows of the palm tree came a snide cackle.

'No man has ever entered the Troll's Lair and lived to tell the tale,' called out Gretchen. 'If you set foot on the Isle of Gula, you will not return. And you are fools to think that even if you do, those treacherous sirens of the deep will return to you *my* emerald.'

'Silence,' said Whitebeard.

'I don't know, Captain,' said Donner. 'She may be right. Where I come from, seeing a mermaid is a bad omen.'

'Until now, who could say they'd seen a mermaid?' replied Whitebeard. 'Only Comet here, and we all thought him mad. Now we have all bathed in their song. Witnessed their heavenly scales. Our ears opened up like empty shells to hear their melodies. Tears of pearl glistened in our eyes as they sang. Your eyes and ears do not deceive you, friends. This omen we can't ignore. How can we call ourselves men of the sea, if we do not answer her call?'

'And if we die trying?' asked Dasher.

'Then at least we've tried. And if we perish and our bodies return to the ocean, we'll do so with pride. Knowing we have our friends beneath the waves to sing for our souls, and do you know what? That might be the greatest treasure of all. Come on, my friends. One last adventure is all I ask. What say you, me hearties?'

'I'm with you, Captain,' shouted Cupid and the other pirates heartily agreed.

'Now, before we set sail again, it is time for us to say goodbye to our guest.' He turned to the elven witch and called out: 'Gretchen, we would like to say it's been a pleasure, but we all know the truth. Still, we don't like to leave our guests empty-handed, so here's a present for you.'

'There's nothing you have that I could want.'

Whitebeard nodded to Dancer and Blitzen and they dumped a large chest at Gretchen's feet. Usually, pirates would leave a marooned shipmate with a flask of water, a pistol and a single bullet, but Captain Whitebeard had other ideas.

'It's everything you need to survive until the next ship comes along.'

And with that, the pirates opened the chest to reveal a mountain of sprouts. Not exactly a Harrods' hamper, you'll agree, and Gretchen retched at the sight of it.

Making their way back to the *Rudolph's Revenge*, the captain delivered the news to the mermaids. The sea maidens sang again their blissful tune and called forth a pod of dolphins to lead the pirates away on their last adventure.

Chapter 16

Alone on her desert island, Gretchen sat and stared out to sea. At first she refused to eat from the smelly chest of Brussels sprouts the pirates had left her, but as hunger gnawed at her belly she reached for one of the rotting green balls and took a bite.

Full of hatred, Gretchen swore she'd find Whitebeard again and her emerald. In fact, she was swearing so much her mouth was drying out in the heat of the day and her thirst for water was matched only by her thirst for revenge. Head down and blinded by the sun, she barely noticed the longboat rowing towards her. Opening her eyes to the hazy horizon, she could just make out a man dressed in white at the helm. Squinting, she saw a squat man next to him, umbrella stretched out in one hand and furiously waving an oriental fan in the other.

Frosty and Oggin strolled up to Gretchen and took a good look at her before speaking.

'What have we here, Oggin? A governor of her very own island, no less.'

'Indeed, sir, but why would Whitebeard waste his time marooning such a sorry-lookin' crone?'

Gretchen scowled.

'If I'm not very much mistaken, Oggin, this pathetic creature is the witch the Spanish captain told us about. Well, you miserable wretch, who are you and why has that old fool Whitebeard left you here?'

'My name is Gretchen, Captain Frost.'

'She knows your name, Captain,' interrupted Oggin.

'I am the most feared pirate captain ever to have sailed the seven seas, Oggin. Everyone knows my name.'

'Others may know who you are, Jack Frost,' began Gretchen. 'But there are few who know your past and only I know your future. I have seen it.'

'Go on,' said Frosty, intrigued.

'Revenge is yours.'

'Oh good,' said Frosty, looking to the skies above. 'I've been so looking forward to it.'

'Untold riches await you.'

'Even better.'

'And … within your grasp is the power to rule *all* mankind.'

There was no denying the glint in Frosty's eye as he listened to the old crone. 'And how do you know these things?' he asked.

'I am no witch, Captain. I'm an elven sorcerer and know the secrets of the past. I alone have the power to deliver what you desire.'

Frosty considered this and laughed. 'You will pardon me, crone, but if you have such magical ability, why are you chained to this tree? Tell me,' he smirked, kicking the chest at her feet, 'do you keep your powers cunningly disguised as Brussels sprouts?'

'Whitebeard stole my power from me and has lost it to the sea. He journeys now to retrieve it. If you let me go, I can show you the way. But we must work together.'

'And why should I work with you? Usually, I force-feed cinnamon to my prisoners until they agree to tell me everything in exchange for a thimble of water.'

'You need me, Jack Frost. Me and my Emerald Envy. The source of all my power.'

'Oggin, send for the cinnamon!'

'Fool!' Gretchen let out a sinister cackle. 'Do not threaten me, Jack Frost. Can't you see we share a foe and I have the power to help you fulfil your destiny? For you are the man in the Elven Prophecy.'

Frosty looked at her suspiciously. 'Wait, Oggin. An Elven Prophecy, no less. Well, let's hear it.'

Gretchen spoke in a grave tone:

'A man who wears a coat of white,
Will be custodian of the light.

With the magic of the Magi's gold;
Endless gifts and power unfold.'

'You know this to be true,' she went on, 'for you have seen my power. It is why you stand here now. The darkness you harbour in your heart is drawn to the emerald's light. Every step of the way it has guided you. Let it guide you now. The path to power is open to you if you destroy Whitebeard and reunite me with my Emerald Envy. Only he can stop you. Only I can help you.'

'And why should I trust you?'

'Because your enemy's enemy is your friend and we both want to see an end to Whitebeard.'

Frosty's one eye stared hard at the elf and his face broke into a villainous smile. 'Very well, Gretchen. We will work together. But cross me at your peril. Deceive me, you die. Betray me, you die. Fail me, you DIE!'

Chapter 17

As night fell Whitebeard kept watch as dolphins led the way to the dreaded Isle of Gula, a fortress island on the sea. Through his telescope, the captain assessed the enormous stone ramparts of the imposing castle. In the fading light, the thick walls, carved out of black volcanic rock, seemed even taller and more impossible to climb. Defended by half a dozen ramparts and twice as many gun turrets, the sea fort looked invincible.

Lurking behind those sinister walls were the most horrible trolls you can imagine. An ugly and oafish bunch, they never washed or brushed their teeth and their pale green faces were all scrunched up like a bulldog chewing a wasp. Each of them had grotesque pot bellies and their beady eyes swivelled above their bulbous green noses, which were constantly on the sniff for children. You might think that with such a highly developed sense of smell, they were aware of their own filthy odours, but of course they weren't. Aye, they were horrible, rank and, worst of all, they loved eating children.

Children were never safe from these hungry beasts. At night the trolls would steal little ones from their beds and swap them with lifeless dolls. Chaining the children in their dungeon, deep at the bottom of the fort, they'd fatten them up to stew them in their boiling cauldron.

Now Whitebeard's task was simple. To save the children from their terrible fate. To break in and rescue the little ones, before the trolls could eat them all. But the walls to the fortress were so high, not even Dancer's skill with a grappling hook could reach the battlements.

'How on earth are we to get inside?' asked Whitebeard, passing his telescope to Comet.

'I know!' said Blitzen. 'We'll use our cannon to blast our way through the walls.'

'Not bad, Blitzen,' said Whitebeard. 'But I fear the walls are too thick and the fort will fire back at us. No, we need something more discreet.'

'I've got an idea,' volunteered Prancer. 'We could use Cupid here as bait. Leave him in a pram outside the fort and it won't be long before the trolls find him and take him inside. Then he can spring his crossbow on the ugly devils and open the gates to let us in. What do you say, Cupid?'

'I'll do it!' said Cupid enthusiastically. 'Let me at them!'

'Not a bad idea,' agreed Whitebeard, 'but I fear it's too risky.'

'Wait, I've got it!' said Vixen. 'We know food is their weakness, so we'll bake them a tasty treat using the ingredients we stole from the Spanish. Donner here could easily whip up a giant pudding or cake. We'll hide inside it with a stack of gunpowder, dynamite and explosives. Then, once we're past the greedy guards and safely in the fort, we'll cut ourselves free, find the children and blow the nasty trolls to smithereens.'

'That's the craziest plan I've ever heard,' said Whitebeard. 'I love it! It'll give them a fright to be sure. Of course, we will need to disguise ourselves as the very best French chefs to give our ruse some clout. Dancer, the French flag and disguises.'

'Aye aye, Captain,' said Dancer, removing his trousers.

Donner surveyed the galley to see what ingredients he had. He needed enough to make something that would be big enough to house a platoon of pyrotechnic pirates. Opening the cases seized from the Spanish, he found mountains of dried fruit, currants, figs and breadcrumbs.

'I can make a figgy pudding. I've got a recipe for the mix and enough to make a pudding with room inside for seven of us.'

The pirates didn't waste time; they rolled up their sleeves to help Donner build the giant pudding. True to form, Blitzen was right beside his mate to lick the bowl whenever he could.

'At last my friends,' said Donner. 'Here's my masterpiece.'

The crew couldn't believe their eyes. There it was, an enormous Christmas pudding, jam-packed with cherries, figs, pears, dates, cranberries, a hair or two from Donner and six barrels of gunpowder.

'Well done, Donner,' said Whitebeard. 'It's a work of art and it'll blow those beastly trolls to kingdom come! Dancer, did you find the disguises we need?'

'Aye, Captain, I did,' said Dancer, producing two tall, white chef's hats and a string of garlic.

'Right, me hearties, Donner and I will dress up as the French chefs. We'll take with us as much food as we can, I have a feeling we're going to be needing it. Gabriel, you and your mates better stay here with the ship, leave this to the professionals. The rest of you, let's be having you in the Christmas pudding.'

The pirates sailed the *Rudolph's Revenge* up to a long jetty, which led to the entrance to the fort. In their matching chef whites, Whitebeard and Donner wheeled the pudding along the winding path and up to the enormous gates where three troll guards stood sentry.

'Oi, what have you got there?' demanded the first guard.

'*It says 'ere, "Mes amis, un pudding for zee Troll's Lair",*' said Whitebeard, putting on his best French accent.

The troll guard took a sniff and softened at the sweet smell of the Trojan treat. 'Mmmm,' he said. 'Follow me.'

The guard led the chefs and their pudding to the keep. The further they went into the lair, the worse the smell. Decaying carcasses and chewed bones littered the dark, dank corridors. Our pirates did not feel well and had to pinch their noses to prevent themselves from being sick there and then.

At last, they entered an enormous banqueting hall decked out with five huge feasting tables.

A dozen fat, foul trolls sat at each one, gobbling away on sausages and dipping them into vats of jelly and custard. They were so busy tucking into their food, they barely noticed the arrival of two French chefs and the giant pudding.

In the middle of the room a huge cauldron bubbled away and there at the head of the largest table, licking juices from a bone, sat the biggest troll you've ever seen. His nasty nostrils twitched and, throwing the finished bone aside, he looked up at Whitebeard.

'I am the Troll King,' he bellowed. 'Who are you? We eat strangers here.'

'*Zis is a wonderful idea, mon ami,*' gushed Donner. '*But might I suggest you allow us to improve your supper wiz our cooking, ah-hon-he-hon.*'

'Nice touch,' whispered Whitebeard. '*Oui, why not add a little garlic? You can eat us certimant, or perhaps we could offer you zis delicious dessert as a gift? If you like zee way it tastes, we will 'elp you wiz your stew. Proof is in zee pudding, non?*'

The huge troll sized them up, fat dripping off his chin. His beady eyes fell on the pudding and his dribbling mouth broke into an ugly grin.

'*We also have zis delicious custard*,' added a nervous Donner.

The Troll King stared hard at the chef. 'I like my puddings toasted. Bring out the brandy and matches at once.'

Chapter 18

Case upon case of brandy was poured over the giant pudding. Inside, the pirates held their breath and exchanged worried looks as Vixen tried to think of a plan. But it was no use, for very soon the pudding would be ablaze. Was this how they were going to die? Entombed within one of Donner's desserts?

'At least we'll be taking those terrible trolls with us,' said Cupid, trying to look on the bright side.

It was hotting up for our pirates all right, and as a flaming torch appeared to ignite the pudding Whitebeard had an idea.

''Old on, 'old on!' bellowed the captain. '*Tis not finished. I insist!*' Sweat trickled down his furrowed brow as he looked at the wicked Troll King. *'You mustn't light it now,'* he pleaded. *'Zee liquor must soak right through.'*

'How long must I wait?' asked the Troll King.

'At least an hour or two.'

'I can't wait that long, I'm hungry now! Bring me out a child as a starter.'

The trolls cheered as two of them went down to bring an unlucky nipper up from the dungeon.

'Please, Monsieur,' insisted Whitebeard. *'Why not sample some of zee other delicious food while you await zee pudding. We do toasted whale, sliced peacock, even swordfish stew.'*

'Tis true,' added Donner. *'Why, we have penguin soufflé and cream teas, or perhaps you'd enjoy this snail and bacon doughnut? Have a taste now, if you please.'*

Trolls may like the taste of children, but they never refuse a free meal and here they had (ahem) two French chefs to cater for their every culinary need. Whitebeard and Donner worked tirelessly and in no time at all had whipped up an incredible feast.

Inside the pudding, Blitzen's belly grumbled loudly.

'What's that noise?' asked the Troll King, tucking into another mince pie.

'*Only zee sweet sound of our cooking, your highness*,' said Whitebeard. '*Can I interest you in an elephant thigh?*'

The captain had to hide his horror as a young boy was brought into the chamber. With his smooth brown skin and open face, the child was the spitting image of Gabriel. Trembling as he was led in, the lad was clearly terrified.

'*Please, let us marinade zee youngster*,' said Whitebeard. '*We must infuse zee little one, mon amis, if he's to taste as good as all zee other food we have delighted you wiz and accompany zee pudding!*'

Whitebeard grabbed the lad, placed him on the table before him and began to smear him from head to toe with raspberry jam.

Luckily, by now the trolls were overfed and, to the smell of blissful aromas, one by one the terrible fiends slipped into sleepy food comas. You know what it's like on Christmas Day, when dinner has been gobbled up and all the grown-ups start falling asleep and breaking wind in front of the telly. Well, the same is true here, my friends, as the terrible trolls entered the land of nod.

'We're here to set you free,' whispered Whitebeard, winking at the young lad. 'Do you know the way to the other children?'

The boy nodded as Donner used his cutlass to carve into the pudding and free the pirates.

'That was close,' said Vixen as she clambered out. 'I wasn't sure how we were going to get out of that one.'

'We're not out of the woods yet,' warned Whitebeard.

And he was right too, for no sooner had the pirates emerged from the pudding than Blitzen's belly began to rumble again, like it had never rumbled before.

'Oh no,' said Blitzen, biting his lip. The loud noise from his tummy was enough to stir the trolls.

'Arrrrgh,' cried out the Troll King, picking up his meat cleaver.

'Trouble, me hearties,' said Whitebeard. 'It's time to give 'em some indigestion! Right, my boy, there's no time to lose. Quickly, lad, which way?'

The boy took Whitebeard by the hand and led the captain deeper and deeper into the lair, leaving the pirates to fight it out with the trolls.

Comet and Cupid overturned a table to defend themselves against the swarm of sluggards. Comet lobbed a grenade or two as Cupid picked off threatening trolls with his crossbow.

Dasher drew his rapier to fend off a bloat of trolls swinging their axes. His effort with the sword was expert enough to run rings around the clumsy clots, allowing Donner to roll out a fuse from the giant pudding. Prancer and Vixen fired their pistols at the roaring devils, but with no time to reload they had to resort to throwing scraps of food to keep them at bay.

Dancer was also under the pump. He'd spiked a couple of trolls with his cutlass, but now the Troll King was hard at him with his cleaver and knocked his sword from his hand. Dancer had no choice but to pick up an abandoned swordfish carcass to use as a makeshift rapier.

Blitzen did his best to liberate his shipmates. Equal in size to even the largest troll, the giant was happily bashing and smashing skulls together. Out cold, the defeated trolls face-planted into vats of vanilla custard as Blitzen moved on to the next batch of pot-bellied devils.

Out of grenades, Comet was left with only a plank of wood from one of the broken tables to defend himself, and in came a trio of trolls with ball and chains swinging above their heads. You have to admire his style as he casually swatted away the flailing blows as if he were opening the batting at Lord's. He's all class, that Comet.

Deep in the belly of the fort, Whitebeard and the little boy entered the dungeon. There, in windowless cells, little children were chained up against the walls. There was no time to spare as Whitebeard pulled out his picklock and began freeing the children.

Prancer and Vixen were the first to appear in the doorway.

'Where are the others?' asked Whitebeard.

'They're coming,' said Vixen. 'We've all made it out of the chamber. The door is shut and Blitzen is doing his best to hold it tight, but we don't have much time.'

'Where's Donner? Did he roll out the fuse?'

'I did,' said Donner, appearing before them. 'But how on earth are we going to get out of here?'

'I know,' said Vixen. 'We climb the chimney.'

Sure enough, there in the dungeon was a giant fireplace with a chimney leading up and out to freedom.

Dancer leapt into the fireplace and swung his grappling hook up the flue. In one swing, he landed his barb into a nook and secured the rope to make their getaway.

'Come on you scurvy knaves, get the children out of here,' Whitebeard ordered.

Rescuing the children, the pirates made their escape. Comet found a fish tank containing three mermaid children and shouldered it.

Whitebeard called out to Blitzen, 'Come, Blitzen, we won't leave you here. Come now! Donner, light the fuse!'

The ship's cook didn't waste time and the spark took instantly, racing its way along the corridor and past where Blitzen lumbered down the hallway.

Running after Blitzen, the trolls saw the flame flick past them.

'Noooooo!' cried out the Troll King. 'You fools, stop that fuse!'

The trolls did their best to turn back and catch up with the racing flame, but they weren't exactly in the best shape after eating twenty-seven meals a day. They had no chance.

Blitzen hauled himself up the rope, with Whitebeard and the lad right behind him. They pulled themselves to freedom just as the pudding was about to blow.

BOOM!

The pudding blasted into angry troll faces as currants and sultanas shot into the air.

The children were hauled to safety as Vixen led them to the ship.

Last out of the chimney were Whitebeard and the little boy, caked in soot from head to toe.

'What's your name?' asked the captain.

'Peter,' he said.

'Okay, Pete, it's time to go!'

Chapter 19

From the *Rudolph's Revenge*, the view of the exploding fortress was spectacular. The blasting bonfire illuminated the sky like an elaborate fireworks display. In the fiery flares, Gabriel and his mates could see the pirates returning with the rescued children. Their faces lit up as they spotted many of them were their own flesh and blood.

'Better release the mermaid children, Comet.' said Whitebeard.

'Aye aye, Captain,' said Comet as he emptied the fish tank into the sea. An awaiting pod of dolphins click-clicked their approval.

Our pirates lifted the children aboard the *Rudolph's Revenge* and into the outstretched arms of their fathers. Reunited at last, the families were cradled in joy and disbelief that they were now safe.

'Peter!' called out Gabriel, and the second he saw him Peter raced towards his dad, throwing his chubby arms around him.

'You've put weight on,' laughed Gabriel, tugging at Peter's cheek.

'That's what happens when you're a prisoner of the trolls, Dad. They were about to eat me when this man saved me.'

'Captain, how can we ever repay you?'

'Think nothing of it, my friend,' said the captain modestly. 'The very least we could do.'

Not all the rescued children found a parent aboard the ship and Whitebeard directed his crew to look after them. To Vixen's amusement, the twins, Holly and Ivy, began following Prancer around as he tried to make sail. A lass called Carol kept Dancer entertained with her song as he jigged away to his heart's content. A young lad called John stuck by Comet at the wheel, keen to learn how the ship sailed.

Elsewhere, a tiny lad called Basil helped Donner in the galley as he prepared some food with the leftovers. Typically, Dasher stayed away from all the kids and found a quiet corner where he kept to himself. Cupid, on the other hand, was delighted to no longer be the titch of the group and, along with Blitzen, made sure the rest of children were entertained.

Prancer and Vixen had the sails up in no time and the merry band set sail into the darkness. Whitebeard promised his new shipmates he'd take them home and set a course with Comet. No sooner had the *Rudolph's Revenge* readied to set sail than a chorus of song sounded from the sea; to the crew's amazement the mermaids had returned with the treasure they'd promised.

'Ancient sailor, our thanks we give,
For fighting so our young might live.
This emerald we return to you.
Your act of kindness has paid what's due.'

The captain reached down to reclaim the glowing emerald from the sea and the mermaids sang one last time, a sweet song that would live on in their hearts forever. The harmony on that Christmas night was something to behold. Looking around at his crew, Whitebeard's heart burst with pride at what he'd done to reunite the families and save them from the terrible trolls. Joy sang up into the night sky and all was well in the world.

The mermaids bid Whitebeard and the pirates farewell and, after a bite or two of Donner's stew, it was time for everyone to take to their bunks.

All but one. For Whitebeard needed a pirate to keep watch that night.

'I know we've all had a long day,' said Whitebeard. 'So the only fair way to decide who will stay up past bedtime is to draw straws.'

The captain stretched out his hand to offer his crew one of eight sticks. Cupid launched in first and pulled out a lengthy looking twig. Dasher and Prancer swiped the next two, both a fraction shorter. Vixen's was shorter still.

Donner's stick was longer than the cabin boy's, as was Comet's. Dancer's looked perilously short. Last but not least, Blitzen drew the last straw. It was barely longer than a thumbnail. He would take watch that night.

Poor old Blitzen. Armed with his enormous blunderbuss and a strong vat of Donner's coffee, the pirate kept his watch.

In the quiet of the night, the *Rudolph's Revenge* rocked gently from side to side and Blitzen did everything he could to stay awake. He lost count of how many times he walked from bow to stern, and he threw in hundreds of squat thrusts and press-ups to boot. Why, he even spent hours thinking long and hard about what he'd do if he retired from being a pirate. Maybe Donner, the powder monkeys and he could join a circus, or even start their own with their share of the plunder.

From a distance you'd be forgiven for thinking Blitzen's eyes were narrowed, keeping an eager watch for the enemy, but look again, my dearios and you'd see his eyelids were falling lower and lower as the toils of the day took their toll on his giant frame. 'WAKE UP, Blitzen!' I can hear you calling. 'WAKE UP!' But it's no use. Blitzen was out like a light and the nasty old *Frostbite* was fast approaching and almost within firing range.

Chapter 20

Below in his cabin, Whitebeard woke suddenly to a strange pecking sensation. It was Robin tapping away at his forehead, trying to get his attention.

'What is it Robin? Trouble?'

The little bird nodded and flew towards the cabin door, signalling for the captain to follow.

Leaping from his bed, Whitebeard pulled on his coat and grabbed his cutlass before stepping out on deck to see Blitzen fast asleep and snoring like a banshee. To Whitebeard, the noise Blitzen made sounded more like cannon. Hang on a tick, it *was* cannon! Turning, Whitebeard saw a flash of orange to his starboard as the *Frostbite* fired its cannon across the waves and into the side of the *Rudolph's Revenge.*

'Blitzen! Get down, man,' shouted Whitebeard as he ducked to take cover from the mighty broadside.

The mast and sails cracked and tore as a fountain of splinters flew in every direction. It was battle stations all right, and Whitebeard rallied his crew to join him.

'Pirates! We're under attack! All hands on deck! Mister Comet, I want you to keep the children well below.'

Racing above, the crew gathered their arms to fight back against the mighty *Frostbite.*

Another blast tore into the side of the *Rudolph's Revenge*, and this time Frosty's assault gave Whitebeard more than a bloody lip. Fires flared all around, as balls of flame engulfed the ship.

'Keep the fire away from the powder,' cried Whitebeard, 'or by the powers, the *Rudolph's Revenge* will soon be *Rudolph's Wreck*!'

No sooner had he uttered those words than a cannonball smashed with furious impact into the side of the ship. Whitebeard gulped as he felt an instant sinking sensation and heard the unmistakable *glug glug glug* of the open hull.

'You fool!' Gretchen turned to Jack Frost. 'If we sink them, we'll lose the emerald.'

Stunned, Frosty's crew looked at each other. They were not used to hearing their captain addressed in such a way, and by the look on Frosty's face the old crone was about to find herself taking the place of a cannonball in the next volley.

After an uncomfortable pause and long hard look at Gretchen, Jack Frost spoke. 'As you wish,' he said with a thin smile. 'We've softened them up well enough. Oggin, prepare to board her. I want to see my Swiss Army Knives in action. Make sure Sawbones, Rabies and Smith are tooled up and ready to go.'

As the guns fell silent, Whitebeard and his crew had only minutes to save everyone from certain death. Under Comet's instruction, Gabriel and his mates used part of a sail to try to fix the gaping hole in the hull, while a chain of pirates formed to bail the leaking water from below to extinguish the fires raging on deck.

'Why have they stopped?' asked Cupid, wiping the sweat and soot from his rosy cheeks.

'If I'm not much mistaken, they're going to board us,' said Whitebeard with a frown. 'Be ready, my friends, this fight is to the bitter end.'

Sure enough, the *Frostbite* had no trouble sailing alongside the *Rudolph's Revenge*. Whitebeard's smaller sloop looked like a toy compared to the fearsome galleon. The popping of Blitzen's smaller guns did little to prevent Frosty's gruesome gang from hurling their grappling irons to the rails to haul the ships closer together.

Jack Frost's men began to board and, now in close quarters, the fighting was fierce.

Blitzen blasted away on his blunderbuss and bashed burly buccaneers with his fists. Dasher fenced French filibusters. Vixen swung at Spanish swordsmen. Dancer dived in to disable dangerous Dutchmen, smashing them over the head with whatever he could find. Prancer's pistols picked off pikemen. Comet's cutlass cut away at cutthroats, and Cupid's crossbow took out troublesome tribesmen.

There was a melee in the mist of cinders, smoke and soot. The mist itself had become a maze and there was no respite to be found in this frenzied haze. To the sound of thumping guns and clashing cutlasses, more villains jumped aboard. You couldn't hear yourself think, my friends, in this storm of sword on sword.

Old enemy eyes met at last as Frosty stepped aboard, brandishing his rapier. Whitebeard raised his cutlass and the ancient foes crossed swords to settle their fiery feud once and for all.

'My old friend, how good of you to drop in and say hello,' said the steely Whitebeard.

'My dear old thing,' spat Frost with a little bow. 'I have come to say goodbye. But not before I have taken from you an eye.'

Frosty's blade twirled skilfully as he darted into the attack. His thrust forward was as fast as lightning, but Whitebeard's reply was just as quick. Frosty sidestepped, then flicked back at his enemy with cool precision. On the back foot, Whitebeard narrowly avoided the point of Frosty's rapier. As the villain swished his blade to go in again, he caught a clump of white whiskers from Whitebeard's cheek.

'Ha!' taunted Frosty with another thrust. 'I'll shear you to death, if it's one hair at a time.'

'Never!' cried Whitebeard, returning with a cut. The two blades were now locked in the air, pointing to the night sky as the men muscled down, pommel to pommel, with all of their force.

The rival captains pushed each other away and raised their swords again to continue the fight.

'You and your pitiful crew are no match for my men,' boasted Frosty, on the front foot again.

Whitebeard was tiring, but swung back at Frosty's sword with everything he had.

The pirates had done well to fight back against the *Frostbite* attack, but now old Frosty had another surprise in store for Whitebeard's crew.

'We're going to cut you to pieces,' snapped Frost. 'Oggin! My Swiss Army Knives!'

Chapter 21

As the Swiss Guard entered the fray, Frosty's host of appalling villains took a step back to enjoy the slaughter. They watched on as the walking dead lined up for battle, the Guards' armour and menacing blades glinting in the moonlight.

Astonished, our pirates looked first at the troop of Switzers and then at each other.

'What on earth is that?' gasped Dasher.

'I don't know, but I love their outfits,' said Dancer. 'Blue, red and yellow. What a combination!'

'I'm not sure I like the look of their steel, though,' pointed out Prancer.

'Maybe their swordplay is rustier than their blades,' said Vixen.

The four friends advanced to receive the first wave. Rapier in hand, Dasher rushed to fend off a trio of zombified guardsmen. Dancer, Prancer and Vixen took on two each.

The arrival of Sawbones, Rabies and Smith spelled more trouble for the *Rudolph's Revenge*. Blitzen and the powder monkeys quickly lined up a cannon to fire at the incoming rascals. But with Smith's giant war-hammer arm, one swing was enough to bash Blitzen's cannon to smithereens. The primates scrambled as Blitzen bravely faced up to Smith with only his fists as weapons.

Elsewhere, Rabies slashed away at Gabriel and his gang, who beat a retreat, allowing the crazed lunatic to unleash his ferocious teeth and claws on the sails, cutting them to ribbons. Donner didn't like the look of this and hurled a loose cannonball at the fiend, knocking his helmet off. But the Switzer began cutting towards him and the ship's cook was forced to peg-leg it to the galley as fast as his crutch could carry him.

From the crow's nest, Cupid let loose his crossbow to fire a well-aimed shot at one of Vixen's assailants, and the first of the guardsmen hit the deck.

'Thank you, Cupid,' Vixen called, to cheers from the other crew.

But Cupid's missile had caught the attention of Sawbones who, with his mechanical buzz saw whirring, sliced into the mainmast like it was salami. The loathsome lumberjack was making short work of the mast when Comet popped up from the hold to fire his two flintlock pistols at the guardsman. The pistol balls hit the Switzer, but only dented his armour. With a howling laugh, Sawbones turned back to his handiwork at the mast. In seconds he brought the wooden pillar crashing down on the deck with an almighty thump that sent poor Cupid flying out towards the sea. Half the mast now hung over the side of the ship like a broken limb. The cabin boy was left stranded at the fishy end; he held on to the basket for dear life as a school of hammerhead sharks circled in the dark waters below.

Not content with felling the mast, Sawbones now turned his attention to Comet in the hold. The devil began burring into the main deck to expose Comet and the terrified children taking refuge below. The youngsters screamed in terror as the saw churned into the roof over their heads.

'Follow me, children!' called Comet, making a run for it along the corridors to hide in the captain's cabin. After bolting the door, Comet got the children to help him push the captain's bed to the doorway as a makeshift barricade.

Rabies was in the galley now and gnashing away as Donner chucked everything, including the kitchen sink, at the vicious hound. But Rabies' razor-sharp teeth made mincemeat of every missile the ship's cook threw at him, grinding away like a brand-new blender. All Donner had left were the powder monkeys' peanuts.

'Any chance you have a nut allergy?' shouted Donner hopefully as he flung the fodder, but it was no use. On Rabies came.

Hammering away like an angry judge, Smith had bashed his way through just about everything Blitzen could find to defend himself. Broken barrels, belaying pins and cutlasses lay in shattered pieces around what was left of the deck. All Blitzen had left was the ship's anchor, which he swung wildly at Smith to hold off the attacking war hammer.

Down below, Sawbones' wheel of death cut through the door to the captain's cabin like a knife through butter. Comet couldn't hear himself think amid the kiddies' screams. They were running out of options. This game of hide-and-seek was not looking good for the little ones. There was no escaping it, the captain's cabin was a dead end.

Speaking of the captain, there he was still fighting it out with Frosty. To be fair to them both, they'd eased off a bit from their cuts and thrusts to take a breather and observe the destruction taking place around them.

'How do you like my Swiss Army Knives, old man?' asked Frosty, pleased as punch.

'I've seen better,' Whitebeard lied, for there was no denying the scale of the devastation.

Reduced to shavings and splinters, the *Rudolph's Revenge* now looked more like a tub of sawdust than a pirate ship. Defeat looked certain.

Chapter 22

Amid the chaos and confusion, no one noticed Gretchen strolling aboard the broken shell of the *Rudolph's Revenge* in search of her emerald. No one, that is, apart from Vixen. She was on to Gretchen and, kicking a bladed guardsman in the crotch, she headed off to face her foe. With a running leap, she hurdled the broken mast and dived on the elven witch, knocking her to the ground.

'I want my emerald, and I'm going to get it back!' spat Gretchen, her bony hands reaching up to strangle Vixen.

'You'll have to get past me first,' answered Vixen, kicking the she-devil away.

'I hoped you'd say that,' cackled Gretchen, pulling a dagger from her dark robe.

At the watery end of the broken mast, Cupid was still in trouble. He tried to climb his way along the long wooden beam, but as he neared the ship, the rocking and rolling of the ocean caused the mast to slip further and further over the side of the ship. It was desperate for the cabin boy as his weight tipped the mast nearer the water. Out swooped Robin to the rescue; the little bird had a line of rope in his beak to aid the youngster. Cupid tied it to the end of his crossbow bolt and fired it into the side of the ship. The cabin boy was just in time and held on for dear life as the mast disappeared from under him and slipped into the depths below.

Breathlessly, Cupid pulled himself up the side of the ship. 'Phew, thank you, Robin.'

In the midships, Dasher, Dancer and Prancer defied all odds against the slashing Switzers. Prancer parried as he was pressed. Dancer box stepped around the savage sabres to land a couple of cuts, but still the guardsmen fought with a ferocious fury. Dasher deftly matched the three-pronged attack he was facing, flicking away the points and outmanoeuvring their advances. But there was trouble to come for the 'The Blade' as he tripped on debris littering the deck and fell to the floor, his sword sent clanging. Prancer saw the terrible trio were about to make Swiss cheese out of his fallen comrade and dived to his aid. Pulling out his questionable Stoompfloggen move, Prancer ducked to the ground behind the Switzers and took a sweeping cut at their calves, bringing the devils to their knees.

'Reckon that was fair, Dasher?' asked Prancer.

'A cut above,' Dasher replied, rolling over to retrieve his rapier and face the oncoming foes.

But before Dasher and Prancer could get to their feet, they were joined on the floor by Dancer who had been knocked to the ground. Eight villains now surrounded the three pirates, blades bent on butchery. Zombie-like faces laughing. Surely, our boys were done for?

'It was a brave effort,' conceded Dasher.

'That it was,' agreed Dancer.

'I thought these Swiss fellas were supposed to be neutral,' pointed out Prancer.

'Stay down!' shouted young Peter at the top of his voice.

He was followed on deck by Gabriel and his chums. They were holding the long slave chain to which they had once been bound. Running at the Swiss Guards, they caught the Switzers around the neck and ran rings around them, choking the guardsmen, their blades powerless against the tight chains. Gabriel's gang dragged the Switzers to the rail and, with one almighty heave, cast the pack of villains over the side of the ship.

'Hooray!' shouted the pirates.

'Thank you,' gasped Dancer.

'That was close,' agreed Prancer, wiping the sweat from his brow.

But right at that moment, no one was sweating it more than Donner. Back in the galley, he was out of projectiles to throw at Rabies and the villain was moving in for the kill. Lying helpless on the floor, Donner closed his eyes as the metal mouth moved towards him. But before Rabies could make a meal out of the ship's cook, a flying fluff ball jumped from an empty shelf in the pantry and dug his claws into the guardsman's face. It was Nero to the rescue, scratching and hissing for all he was worth. Unable to brush the cat away without tearing at his own face, Rabies tried instead to shake the moggy off, but it was no use; this fierce feline had his claws in deep. Staggering back, Rabies tripped towards the rail. Donner was back on his feet now and, armed with only his crutch, he hobbled towards the Switzer.

'Jump, Nero. Now!' cried the cook as he swung his crutch like a baseball bat to strike a home run into Rabies' chops. The blow was big enough to send the guardsman flying overboard to join his comrades in the ocean below.

The fight between the heavyweights raged on as Smith and Blitzen battled it out at the bow. Ducking and diving, Blitzen had done well to escape the hammer blows. Swinging his weighty

anchor, he even landed a hook of his own to Smith's anvil jaw. But Smith copped it on the chin and hit back by smashing his murderous mallet down hard onto Blitzen's chest. The force sent the pirate reeling backwards to the brass mount of a broken cannon. The Switzer took advantage of the moment by pinning the giant up against the gun, choking him with his war-hammer arm. Blitzen's face went redder and redder; he was about to pass out when all of a sudden he saw a look of surprise on Smith's face.

The powder monkeys had come to his rescue and pulled the guardsman's pants down. Using some gun cartridges and a ramrod, the cheeky chimps had breached Smith's breeches and loaded him with an explosive wedgie. With the fuse lit, sparks scorched the Switzer's bare bottom. There was nothing for it but for Smith to jump into the sea and take his chances with the hammerhead sharks.

Down below, Sawbones' circle of doom cut into the cabin.

'Get back, children, quickly. Hide behind the treasure chest,' said Comet. The pirate's courage was second to none as he stood up to the buzz saw with his cutlass, but it was shattered to pieces the second it touched the spinning disc. Comet crashed to the floor, losing his spectacles in the tumble. Half blind, he crawled as fast as he could towards the blur of the wooden chest and, grabbing at anything he could, he hurled the contents at his enemy. Bars of gold and bags of silver were flung at the mechanical maniac, but nothing could stop the guardsman and his nasty instrument of death. The whirling saw moved within inches of Comet's head, and he blindly reached for something to protect his face. As the children screamed, Comet held up a chunky diamond as a shield. Sawbones chuckled as he went in for the kill. But the last laugh was on him. The diamond was so tough, it shattered the spinning buzz saw. Sawbones' mouth gaped open in disbelief.

'Quickly, children,' said Comet. 'Pack his pants with plunder.'

Gathering themselves, the kids flew at Sawbones, filling his pockets and pants with heavy gold bars and bags of silver.

'Forgive me, old chap,' said Comet. 'It's time for us to pay you back, with interest.'

With all his might, Comet pushed Sawbones head first through the cabin window and into the watery silence of the deep blue sea.

It had been a solid effort all round from the crew aboard the *Rudolph's Revenge*. Even Whitebeard finally had the measure of that menace Frosty. With a solid sabre cut and an almighty heave, Whitebeard sent Frosty's rapier flying and the villain put his hands in the air. But on the other side of the deck, Gretchen had gained the upper hand over Vixen who was on her knees. The elf pulled back Vixen's hair and held a dagger to her throat.

'Where is my emerald, girl?'

'I'll never tell you. Never.'

'You might not, but I think we know someone who will. Captain Whitebeard!' cried Gretchen to the old sailor. 'Hand me back my emerald, Captain, or by the stars, I'll end her life now. What's it to be?'

'No, don't give it to her!' cried Vixen.

Whitebeard looked at Vixen and then at Gretchen. With a furrowed brow, the captain dropped his cutlass, pulling the emerald from his pocket. It shone brightly in his hand as he took a deep breath.

'Here,' he said, tossing it to the witch. 'Now let her go.'

Gretchen let go of Vixen's hair to catch the glimmering green stone. Once it was back in her hands, the Emerald Envy filled the night sky with a burst of shining light. Blinded by the brightness, all the pirates could make out was the chilling sound of a familiar and sinister cackle.

Chapter 23

Shimmering as she stood in the shadows, Gretchen appeared before the pirates in all her glory. No longer an old wretch, her beauty was a sight to behold. The wrinkles had vanished, replaced by smooth pale skin. But the eyes were the same moss-green pools of hate. From a pocket in her robe, the elf pulled out a rancid pair of Brussels sprouts and held them up for all to see.

'Sprouts once you gave me,
The only thing I ate.
Now behold a green-eyed monster,
Sprouting from my hate.'

The stinky sprouts glowed green as Gretchen cast her spell and threw them into the ocean. Spewing and spluttering, the water bubbled away like the contents of a slimy cauldron. The pirates held their breath in horror as a monster of ferocious size emerged from the sea. First came it's huge green gargoyle head, then it's bulging body and gargantuan limbs. The monster grew bigger and bigger until it was so huge it dwarfed what was left of the *Rudolph's Revenge*. The terrible creature let out a devastating screech as it cast its sprouty green eyes on all before him.

Now, from his front row seat, you may think Jack Frost was loving what he saw and yelling at Oggin to bring the popcorn. But Gretchen's monster was so terrifying, not even he was game enough to stick around. He and his crew made a dash for it back to the *Frostbite* to make their getaway.

'Farewell, Whitebeard,' he said with a nasty laugh. 'Nothing can save you now.'

Gretchen too cackled away as she followed Frosty with her jewel in hand and left

Whitebeard and his shipmates to await their desperate fate.

All hopes were dashed for our crew. As the screeching monster smashed away at the remnants of the *Rudolph's Revenge*, our pirates could do nothing but hide in what was left of the hold below.

'We're perished this time for sure,' wheezed Dasher.

'There must be something we can do?' said Cupid.

'I'm afraid this time Dasher could be right,' said Whitebeard. 'I have failed us. I'm sorry, me hearties. But I for one am not going to give up without a fight.' The captain raised his sword as he prepared to step back out on deck to face the green-eyed monster.

'If only we had some magic we could use against it!' said Blitzen.

'Wait, Captain! Blitzen, you're a genius,' said Vixen. 'I've got it, Captain! A plan to save us all.'

Vixen ran to her sea chest and pulled out the mistletoe Gretchen had used to make her love charm. Looking at the sprig of berries, she doubted for a second if this would work. Could she really get a green-eyed monster to fall in love with her? Well, it was better to try and fail than never try at all. It was time to find out.

'Here, Captain,' she explained. 'Gretchen once gave me this magic mistletoe. She said it can make anyone fall in love with me.'

Vixen reddened as she told her shipmates how the magic might work.

'You expect that great green-eyed monster to fall in love with you?' asked Prancer. 'It can't be done. He's way out of your league!'

'Aye, well, it's worth a shot,' said Vixen. 'Right, Cupid, take your crossbow and this mistletoe to the highest point on the ship. Then, when I give the signal, fire it above the monster's head. Then I'll launch myself at him and kiss him on the lips. With a bit of luck, he'll fall in love with me.'

'This is a terrible plan, Vixen,' said Whitebeard. 'But it's the only plan we've got. Pirates, let us create a distraction to help Cupid and Vixen get into place.'

'You're actually going to kiss that thing?' said Prancer.

'That's right, now where did I put my lipstick? I'm going to want to look my best!'

Well, if you thought those devilish Switzers had made a mess of the *Rudolph's Revenge*, that was nothing compared to the destructive power of the green-eyed monster. The vessel looked nothing like a ship any more, and now the enormous beast lifted it out of the water like a toy boat.

With a roaring battle cry, Whitebeard led the pirates from the hold to launch an attack on the screeching monster, but with a flick of his fingers the beast sent the men flying like balls breaking on a pool table.

But the distraction had worked; Cupid managed to get into position between the antlers on the figurehead of the *Rudolph's Revenge* and took aim with his crossbow.

'Don't miss, Cupid,' Vixen pleaded under her breath. 'Please don't miss.'

Eyes narrowing to take aim, the cabin boy steadied his hand and let loose his crossbow. The mistletoe soared higher and higher towards the monster's head and the shot looked good. Then a gust of wind caught hold of the sprig and it shot past the unlikely Romeo.

'Now we're done for,' gasped Vixen.

But, from nowhere, Robin appeared and collected the magic mistletoe in his beak. What a catch from the redbreast. Now the little bird circled the green-eyed monster's head. The sprouty devil didn't like this one bit and looked set to give Robin a belting blow. But Robin soared higher and higher into the sky to deliver the monster a little Christmas gift of his own.

Taking aim with his bottom, Robin pooped a dropping right into the monster's left eye. Some say it brings you good luck to receive such a present from a bird, but you wouldn't have known it from the way the monster went berserk.

With Robin holding the mistletoe in place, it was now or never for Vixen.

'Come here, you handsome monster! I've always loved green eyes.'

Jumping towards the monster, Vixen went in for the kill, lunging at him like it was the stroke of midnight at a New Year's Eve party. No one was more surprised by Vixen's desperate dive than the unloved green-eyed monster. Lips locked onto lips and the sprouty fellow couldn't believe his luck as she kissed him.

Vixen's passion overwhelmed the monstrous creature. All at once he forgot who or what he was and he placed the *Rudolph's Revenge* down gently upon the waves. It was a brave effort from Vixen, who pretended not to notice the nasty smell of sprouty seaweed or the big green bogey hanging down from his enormous schnozz.

The monster picked up Vixen and held her tenderly between his fingers, before giving her a big hug and placing her with great care back on the *Rudolph's Revenge*. Besotted, the sprouty eyes followed Vixen as he gazed lovingly at his girl.

But like many a fleeting romance, this wasn't to last long. Blitzen was ready and waiting with his blunderbuss. He fired off a booming blast and it caught the green-eyed monster right between the eyes, blowing his head to smithereens. Sprouty seaweed filled the sky and covered the crew and deck of the *Rudolph's Revenge*.

Caked in green goo, Vixen lay flat on her back.

'Are you trying to make me jealous?' said Prancer, stretching out an arm to help Vixen to her feet.

'Did it work?' she asked, grabbing his hand.

Prancer picked her up and gave her an almighty hug. Even though she was exhausted, covered from head to toe in green goo and smelt like a potty, at that moment she'd never felt so happy.

'*Heave-to, my little deario,*' sang Whitebeard under his breath. '*Heave-to.*'

Chapter 24

The first light of a new day dawned on Whitebeard as he kept a lonely watch on deck. The captain had decided to keep watch himself that Christmas night, to let his crew rest after the ordeal they'd experienced at the hands of perilous enemies.

In the glory of the morning sky, the candy-floss clouds turned pink. Taking a deep breath, Whitebeard inhaled the sweet air of the Caribbean as the bitter taste of gunpowder lingered on his tongue. The rolling of the sea picked up as the breeze grew stronger in the early light. The captain shut his eyes and listened carefully to the sound of the sea. Was it the lolling of laughter or a rasp of applause he could hear as the waves crashed against the wooden carcass of his ship?

'What have I done, my friend?' he muttered to Robin, perched loyally on his shoulder. 'What have I done? Why, I've handed over the Emerald Envy to that knave Jack Frost and the wicked Gretchen. A more terrible trinity I cannot imagine, and now who knows what fiendish villainy they have in store for us all? What would my Mary think of me?'

The little bird chirped a cheerful song to lift Whitebeard's spirits. As he listened, the captain couldn't help but think back to the moment he rescued the children from the trolls and delivered the mermaids back to the open arms of the sea. Why, he'd even seen Dasher and Prancer shake hands at the end of their struggles against Frosty, the Swiss Army Knives and the green-eyed monster. Surely, he had done something right?

With the sun rising higher now, the captain began to feel better as he looked towards the golden horizon.

'Thank you, my little friend. You are quite right,' he whispered to the redbreast. 'This is just the beginning.'

The pirates knew the ship was a wreck when they'd turned in for the night. Now, as they clambered out of their hammocks to join their captain on deck, the scale of the destruction was clear for all to see. The *Rudolph's Revenge* looked more like a raft than a pirate ship.

'Well, me hearties, what have you to tell me?' asked Whitebeard.

'We regret to tell you, Captain,' said Prancer, 'we are all at sea.'

'We've no sail,' said Vixen.

'We've no mast,' said Cupid.

'We've no guns or powder,' said Blitzen.

'We've no food,' said Donner.

'We don't really know where we are, either,' said Comet.

'Or where we are going,' added Dancer.

'Aye, Captain, and we've lost all the booty, loot and plunder,' said Dasher.

Whitebeard stroked his beard as he looked around at his bleary-eyed crew and then at the men and children they'd saved. Gabriel stood with his arm around his son and the pair directed warm smiles at the captain that made his heart fill with pride.

'We do have each other,' said Peter, 'thanks to you.'

'He is right,' said Gabriel. 'We are still alive and we have our freedom. For that alone, we thank you. We will help you, Captain. We can help you rebuild your ship and fight on. It is a miracle that we are all still alive. It is a miracle that you saved us and our children. We will never be able to repay you for what you have done. To us, you truly are a saint. You are what we call Santa.'

And with that, Gabriel's gang and the children began chanting in a low, rhythmic hum.

'Santa, Santa, Santa,' they sang.

The captain was overcome with emotion.

'My friends,' he said, putting his arms around his nearest shipmates, 'you are too kind and I alone cannot take credit for the endeavour and sacrifice of this crew. How could we have survived if not for Dasher's skill with the blade, Dancer's bravery, Prancer's fight or Vixen's cunning? Where would we be now if it were not for Comet's courage, Cupid's aim, Donner's pudding or Blitzen's might? My dear friends, you have all helped us to live to fight another day. Now, I fear the fight against our foes has only just begun. It will take great strength and character to overcome our fears and meet the challenges and unspeakable dangers that lie ahead. But I know that if we stay true to ourselves and stand tall, we can prevail. We must. I know we can do it, for as young Pete says, we have each other and that's what counts.'

Exhausted though they were, the crew cheered and embraced one another.

'Now, Donner, are you quite sure we haven't got anything left to eat? Anything at all?' asked Whitebeard.

The ship's cook shrugged and, scraping up a sludge of green goo from the deck, turned back to his shipmates with a hopeful smile.

'Sprouts anyone?'

Epilogue

What a Christmas it's been my friends,
For our crew on the *Rudolph's Revenge*!
Encountering mermaids, trolls and perilous foes;
Yes, they've plenty to avenge.

Now in the captain's cabin,
They sit and laugh and share
What little food they've left to eat,
And the stories of their scare.

Watch now festive friendships flourish
And good times had by all.
They put the Advent in adventure,
These pirates big and small.

I know you still have questions …
And there's plenty still to come.
Like all Christmas feasts and banquets,
There's leftovers before we're done.

When do we meet Rudolph the reindeer
And why's his nose so red?
What of flying sleighs and stockings?
Well, now it's time for bed.

Many chapters more await you.
Many battles more to come.
There's so much more in store, my friends,
Before Santa's story's won.

Whitebeard may have saved the kids,
But with Frosty and Gretchen still at large
There's an ocean of events to bring you,
But for now, let us recharge.

Sleep now and enjoy your Christmas Day,
Make merry and be glad
Of all your friends and loved ones.
Your family really ain't that bad.

Heave-to, my little dearios,
Enjoy all the festive cheer.
A very Merry Christmas, friends,
And have a Happy New Year!

Ahoy there matey!
More adventures await you.

WHITEBEARD

will be back.

Find out more and join our crew at

www.whitebeardbook.com

You'll receive exclusive offers and
updates and be the first to know when
the *Rudolph's Revenge* returns.

FOLLOW US ON:

@whitebeardbook

facebook.com/whitebeardbook

Glossary

Ahoy: a sea call used to get someone's attention.

Aye: pirate for 'yes'.

Barbary pirate: a North African pirate of Ottoman origin.

Belaying pin a fixed wooden pin used to secure ropes.

Bilge: the bottom of a ship.

Booty: stolen goods.

Bow: the front of a ship.

Broadside: the firing of all guns on one side of a ship.

Buccaneer: a pirate of Caribbean origin.

Canonised: officially declared to be a saint.

Corsair: a pirate of Mediterranean origin.

Cutlass: a short sword used by sailors.

Fetters: chains used to secure prisoners.

Freebooter: a Dutch word for pirate.

Filibuster: a Spanish word for pirate.

Galley: a ship's kitchen.

Grog: a drink made with rum and water.

Heave-to: to slow down or stop.

Longboat: a large boat launched from sailing ships.

Marlinspike: a metal spike used as a tool.

Marooning: to leave a victim on a deserted island.

Mes Amis: French for 'my friends'.

Mon Ami: French for 'my friend'.

Oui: French for 'yes'.

Salud: Spanish for 'cheers'.

Sangria: an alcoholic punch.

Sea rover: a sailor or pirate.

Shanty: a sailor's song.

Slops: trousers.

Starboard: the right side of the ship when facing the bow.

Stern: the back of a ship.

Stoompfloggen: duelling contest played with wooden cutlasses.

Squonk: an ugly mythical creature.

Windward: the direction upwind or the direction from which the wind is coming.

M.C.D. Etheridge

Matthew Campbell D'Arcy Etheridge is a writer, journalist and TV producer.

WHITEBEARD is his first book.

Originally from the White Cliffs of Dover in the UK, Matt now lives in Sydney, Australia.

Matt's favourite thing about Christmas is spending it with his family, friends and loved ones.

He doesn't like Brussels sprouts.

Olivia Ong

An animator by day, Olivia loves to spend her spare time drawing.

Olivia grew up in Sydney's inner west and went to Campsie Public School. She now lives in Melbourne.

Her favourite thing about Christmas is making handmade gifts for her family and loved ones.

Lightning Source UK Ltd.
Milton Keynes UK
UKHW012328021218
333372UK00005B/45/P